William Thomas Johnson

Twelve Years of a Soldier's Life

From the Letters of Major W.T. Johnson of The Native Irregular Calvary

William Thomas Johnson

Twelve Years of a Soldier's Life
From the Letters of Major W.T. Johnson of The Native Irregular Calvary

ISBN/EAN: 9783337016449

Printed in Europe, USA, Canada, Australia, Japan

Cover: Foto ©Raphael Reischuk / pixelio.de

More available books at **www.hansebooks.com**

TWELVE YEARS

OF

A SOLDIER'S LIFE

FROM THE LETTERS OF

MAJOR W. T. JOHNSON

OF THE NATIVE IRREGULAR CAVALRY

EDITED BY HIS WIDOW

LONDON

A. D. INNES & CO.

BEDFORD STREET

1897

CONTENTS.

TWELVE YEARS OF A
SOLDIER'S LIFE.

CHAPTER I.

EARLY DAYS. 1827–1849.

IN a battle men hold varied stations. Some are great leaders, whose names are on the lips of every one ; others, the fearless spirits who press on in front. There are those, again, who do good service in the rear ; and the day may be lost or won, by the behaviour at a critical moment, of some one person that nobody knows of, but whose influence for good or evil has been vital.

These turning-points have happened in many a crisis of history ; and as we rejoice in a great victory, or honour the name of a great commander, let us not forget that the battle may have been won, and

B

the leader supported, by the heroism or presence of mind of men, of whom the world knows absolutely nothing. So will it be seen in the following sketch.

William Thomas Johnson was born at Enborne Rectory, Newbury, Berks, on March 14th, 1827. He was the youngest of the three children of the Rev. Charles Thomas Johnson, Rector of Enborne and of Hampstead Marshall. The family has for some centuries been settled in Lincolnshire, and the Grammar Schools of Uppingham and Oakham were founded by an ancestor, Archdeacon Robert Johnson, in the reign of Edward VI. The hereditary grand trusteeship of both these schools, is always held by the head of the Johnson family. Another ancestor went to America, and was the founder of the city of Boston, which he named after his old county town. The grandfather of "Billy" Johnson (as he was always called) was a captain in the army, but afterwards took Holy Orders, and was for some years Rector of Wistanstow, in Shropshire. He married Anna Rebecca, sister of the sixth Lord Craven, and had three sons and four daughters. His eldest son, William, afterwards General Johnson, succeeded to the family estate of Wytham-on-the-Hill, Lincolnshire. The second son, Henry, held for many years the rectories of Lutterworth and Claybrook, of which it will be remembered John Wyclyff was rector. The third son, Billy's father, was educated at Shrewsbury, and at Brasenose College, Oxford, where he gained the Craven Scholarship, and was afterwards Rector of Enborne and Hampstead Marshall, Berks, on the presentation of his cousin, the Earl of Craven.

Of the daughters, two only were married—the eldest, Harriet, to General Sir John Dalrymple, afterwards eighth Earl of Stair, and the youngest, Selina, to the Rev. Henry Williams.

The Rector of Enborne was a courteous, high-bred gentleman, and an excellent parish priest. He was fond of sport and of farming, but never indulged these tastes to any extent after his ordination. He devoted himself to his parochial work ; setting on foot schools in both parishes, classes for lads, and cottage readings, which in those days were quite the exception in the country.

In 1817 he married Lucy Anne, youngest daughter of Sir John Blois, Bart., of Cockfield Hall, and Grundisburgh, Suffolk, where they had been seated from the time of Henry VII. Mrs. Johnson was one of the most popular and charming women in the neighbourhood. She survived her husband many years, living at Enborne Rectory with her eldest son, Charles Augustus, who succeeded his father as rector in 1848. Billy's only sister, Lucy Anne Maria, married, in 1855, her cousin, Frederick Palmer-More-wood, Barrister-at-Law.

The parish of Enborne, in which Billy's childhood was spent, is described in Domesday-book as Ane-burne, or Taneburne, and one of its manors was con-veyed to Thomas Chaucer, a son of the poet. It is historically interesting as being the scene of the first battle of Newbury, which was fought near the Rectory, and many of the slain were buried in Enborne church-yard. A letter was said to have been written by Oliver Cromwell to the then rector, in the following terms: "I desire that the dead of my army be buried in your churchyard. Disobey me at your peril."

A very remarkable man, Nicholas Ferrar, after-wards famous as the founder of the Anglican Monastery at Little Gidding, was at school at En-borne Rectory with the Rev. Robert Brooke, a pro-nounced Puritan of that time.

The other parish, Hampstead Marshall, belonged formerly to the Earls-marshal of England ; hence its name. It passed through many hands till it was bought, in 1610, by the great soldier Sir William

Craven. He had a romantic attachment for the beautiful Queen of Bohemia, and is said to have built a fine mansion in the Park, somewhat after the style of Heidelberg Castle, to gratify her. It was unfortunately burnt down in 1718, and only the stately entrance-gates are now standing. The present house was built by Lord Craven in 1720.

Billy and his brother and sister had a strong love of driving, riding, and outdoor life and sport. He also inherited from his father a talent for mechanical work, building and carpentering, which he developed in after years.

At the age of ten he was sent to Mr. Meyrick's school at Ramsbury, in Wiltshire, well known in those days, where his brother had been for some time. Billy was there four years, and brought back, according to his father's journal, "a good character for all but books." He was very popular as a lad; a general favourite.

In February, 1841, his father took him to Rugby. The son of an intimate friend, Mr. Hughes, of Donnington, the future author of " Tom Brown's Schooldays," was there in the sixth form, and he chose Billy for one of his fags. The late Tom Hughes wrote recently about him: "He was some five years younger, but I always knew him well in those days, and was much attracted to him, as he was one of the brightest boys I ever remember. I fancy this was the reason he was sent to Rugby, where I was a sixth-form boy, in 1841 and 1842, and his father and mother knew that I should look after him. So I did, though no small boy ever needed it less, as he got on at once with his school-fellows. I chose him as one of my fags, of whom each sixth-form boy had four in those days; excused him all study fagging, and helped him, when he asked me to do so, with his lessons, which, so far as I remember, was very seldom. Perhaps I may have neglected this part of my duty, for he was low in the school, and had no vocation for the classics. Had the modern system been in force, I have no doubt that such a bright boy would have found some study which would have attracted him. I was only there with him for a year, and unluckily lost sight of him, and only saw him at long intervals, though I followed his career with great interest and sympathy. His marked characteristic in those early days was his perfect temper: I don't think I ever saw him put out, or moping. I wish I could give you more than these general impressions, but cannot call to mind any more definite impressions, except, by the way, that he was called 'Billy,' and never had any nickname that I can remember. You and his sons have every reason to be proud of his career."

Billy was in Bonamy Price's house, and his own modest account of himself was, " I learnt to fish and swim at Rugby." But apart from books he learnt a great deal. He was under the influence of Dr. Arnold, and every one knows what this influence was. Reverence, honour, truth, and courage were taught by him, and in the after career of the men we read of in the "Military and Naval Records of Rugbeans," we see evidences of the teaching of the great Head Master. The Duke of Wellington is said to have remarked that " the battle of Waterloo was won on the playing field of Eton ; " and Billy's after career bears splendid testimony to his early training. "Well to the front" at Inkerman, charging the enemy's gun almost unsupported at the Alumbagh, fetching in the wounded during the siege of Lucknow ; assuredly the seed sown at Rugby bore its fruit.

His letters written home from India show that, as a young man and keen sportsman, he was faithful to early teachings. He wrote : "I don't hunt on Sundays ; not that I don't do many worse things, I am sorry to say ; " and again : " I don't shoot on Sundays ; made it a rule a long time ago." He had a great veneration for the Bible, and for the authority of religion ; a strong faith in prayer (he often used to say he knew his mother's prayers had saved him in many a battle and a peril), and a great respect for Sunday. His reverence at church was remarked all through his life. It was the simple faith and practice of a soldier.

In June, 1842, Dr. Arnold died. The impression on the minds of the boys was overwhelming, and Billy used often to speak of the panic in the school on that Sunday morning, when the news went round " Arnold is dead."

On leaving Rugby, Billy was sent to Brussels, to the school of a Dr. Friedlander, to study modern languages. He had previously had a strong wish to enter the Royal Navy, but at his age this was not thought advisable, and his father determined to prepare him for India. He remained at Brussels until March, 1845, and brought home very good reports ; but he was not the sort of boy to care for a foreign school, being so intensely English in his tastes and ways. The school he used to call " the prison," and would tell a story in after years of how the boys once ran away in a body as far as Waterloo. He learnt, however, a fair amount of French and German ; and on his return to England his father sent him to

Kensington School, which at that time had a reputation as preparatory for India, and gave special
facilities for the study of Hindustani. He was in
the house of Mr. Jermyn, who wrote to his father:
"His conduct is everything I could wish. He is
industrious, steady, and well-conducted, and all
the masters speak well of him." He obtained prizes
in Hindustani and drawing, and left with a high
character.

In March, 1846, his father made arrangements with
Major Oliphant for his going to India, and he was
sworn in at the India House on April 23rd, and
sailed from Southampton on May 2nd, 1846. His
father wrote in his journal of May 1st: "A beautiful
rifle has arrived from Lord Craven to dear Billy;"
(Lord Craven was his godfather) "his last day with
us! how very sad!" And on May 2nd, he wrote:
"Our dear boy is gone, and it is so like death, words
cannot describe my sorrow." From this date to that
of his own death, (which happened suddenly in June,
1848,) his father never spoke of "dear, dear Billy," but
with affection and regret; indeed, he never seemed to
get over his son's going to India (which in those days
was a very different thing to what it is now), and he
had a great horror of the country and climate. Billy
was deeply attached to his father, and the shock of

his death was a very real sorrow to him. He wrote at that time to his mother (August, 1848): "The dreadful, unlooked-for news reached me on the morning of the 7th inst. The shock to you all must have been nearly as sudden as it was to me. . . . We must not murmur against the Almighty Wisdon that has been pleased to take to Himself the most affectionate of fathers; and on our part it is almost a selfish feeling to mourn for one that we well know has gone to a far happier world; but it is very hard to bear up against the severest sorrow that could have been sent." . . . "There is a great deal of work in the shape of duty going on now, which perhaps is a good thing for me, as it helps to keep my mind employed for the time; but I find it difficult, when alone, to keep my thoughts from wandering amongst you, which makes me more and more unhappy. Every one has been uncommonly kind to me, and sympathizes with me, almost as if they had known the beloved one for whom we mourn."

On his arrival at Bombay, in June, 1846, Johnson was kindly received and entertained by his cousin, Captain Tom Turner, of the Engineers, who had married a daughter of Sir Herbert Compton; and he was gazetted to the 6th Bombay Native Infantry in the autumn of this year. Colonel William Macan was commandant of the regiment, which was stationed at Sattara. His particular friends in it were Captain Glasspoole, a Norfolk man, and Jervis Harpur, "Jarvey," as he was always called, now General Harpur. It was at Sattara that he first became acquainted with Outram and his wife, who were there at that time ; and he was again thrown with them, when, in January, 1848, the regiment was moved to Baroda, the capital of the territory of His Highness the Guikwar. He wrote, on the march for Mahableshwur :

"As far as this, I have enjoyed my march particularly, and am living as comfortably as if I were in a house. I always send my tent and two or three servants on overnight, so as to have it pitched and ready by the time we come up in the morning, and keep a small rowtie to sleep in. Glasspoole, of ours, is living with me in the same tent, as he does not possess one of his own ; he is a very jolly, good-natured fellow, and we get on famously together, considering it is our first march. We march down the other side of the ghat to-morrow morning, and shall be in Bombay about the 20th."

On arriving at Bombay he changed his river-boat for a larger one, to bring him up to Cambay. In his own words : "I hoisted the main-sail to the wind and

wished for morning, but all the sails in the world
would never have persuaded such an old bucket as I
was in to move more than fourteen miles a day; but
notwithstanding that mine was such a slow coach, it
was one of the fastest of the whole fleet, fifteen in
number, beating the adjutant's by several lengths and
the commanding officer's by three days. It is four
marches between the place we landed at and Baroda.
I was agreeably surprised with the beauty of the
country, which strikes one particularly coming out
of the Deccan, though Guzerat is as flat as a pan-
cake; there are parts in it which almost resemble a
gentleman's park in England."

In 1848 he wrote to his sister, that he had had his
first attack of fever, and described it as " a sensation
of a blacksmith's shop, or iron steamer manufactory
going on in my head; but four dozen very hungry
leeches soon put me all to rights." He writes of his
furniture at this time as consisting of " a couple of
chairs, a brace of tables, two candlesticks, two hog-
spears, and a book-shelf." In a letter to his father
he describes his household : " I am obliged to keep
nine servants : one to wait upon me at dinner ; one
to take care of my clothes and kit ; another to
clean knives and shoes, sweep the house, and so on.
One man to take care of the pony, a dog boy, a

washerman, a tailor, a man that calls himself a gardener, and lastly a 'puggy,' which being interpreted means a watchman, who is supposed to keep thieves out of your house at night, but in truth is nothing more nor less than a robber himself. Every officer in camp is obliged to have one of these beings, otherwise he would have everything walked away with in no time. It is a curious piece of policy, you will say, keeping a robber to keep others away, but it is the case; and if I were to discharge my puggy to-morrow, he would tell his caste, and my house would be cleared out in a month or two ; and if he could not succeed in this, he would catch me out shooting some day and give me a bit of knife, or pot me with an arrow from behind a hedge, so I think it best to keep at peace with this canine race! The latter part of last month (March) gave us a specimen of Baroda weather; we were just able to keep ourselves warm, the thermometer being only 139°! It was the hottest ten days I have ever experienced, and the atmosphere is so extremely moist."

A little later he wrote : " The hot winds are begining to blow, and all sorts of artificial means are adopted to keep the house in a bearable state— tatties, thermantidotes, and punkahs; but as you must have a very small idea what these things mean, it will be as well to tell you that the tatty is a sort of lattice frame made of bamboo, in which is placed a grass called cuscus, and put in the doorway or window, and kept constantly wet, with the wind blowing through it. The thermantidote is a sort of winnowing machine, to make artificial air. I can't afford any of these luxuries, but most of the bigwigs have got them. My house is 96° in the shade in the daytime."

At Baroda Johnson's chief friends were Colonel and Mrs. Hale, and the two brothers John and William Leckie, in the 13th and 22nd Regiments; also the Outrams, until they left for Deesa in September. He spoke of Outram's wishing all the officers to get a banquet given by the Guikwar of Baroda, which he described in a letter to his sister. "His Highness sent carriages for us; a great improvement on the elephants, which generally take us on these occasions. The first entertainment was some nautching, in which two very uninviting black females attempted a *pas de deux*, not quite *à la Cerito*, or Fanny Essler, as you may imagine. They danced and sang, or made a noise, at the same time, and wore nuts in their noses, which had a very unbecoming effect. The dinner was the most satisfactory part,

I thought, and some capital ice after dinner. Next to this came some fireworks, but the attention of most of us was taken away from these by the native officer commanding the Guikwar's troops, who was the worse for a couple of bottles of champagne. The way he tumbled over his men and into the lamps was very ridiculous. The first shower fell on the 27th of last month (June), and the growth of the grass was the most ridiculous thing I ever saw, for not having had any rain since October last, you can fancy the dusty look of the country; but two mornings after the first shower everything was perfectly green."

In the beginning of 1849 he took a house at Baroda with his friend Harpur, "a gentleman," he writes, "in blood and manners, which is an article you don't always meet with in these parts. We have not fallen out yet, and the chances are we shall get on very well. He has the best part of the house; I gave him his choice, on condition I might choose the stabling." Johnson had an Arab horse, called "The Arab's Choice," to which he was devoted, and which carried him perfectly. This horse he often mentions in his letters ; he was afterwards lost, with all his other possessions, in the Mutiny, a loss he never ceased to deplore.

The neighbourhood of Baroda was famous for pig-sticking, of which he was very fond. He describes an expedition with Harpur, Battye, and some other friends : " We killed five altogether in the two days' hunting—three boars and two sows ; Battye stuck two of the boars, and I the other. Lodwick, our Brigade Major, and Graham stuck a sow each.   Harpur and Smith were both on indifferent horses, but rode famously ;" and again, of another hunt : " I got one boar to my own cheek ; he was the largest we killed, and such fine tushes, about seven inches long, and as sharp as the point of a pin.   He knew how to use them, too, for he ripped my horse (the dear little bay) slightly, and another dreadfully—tore its leg entirely to pieces ; I never saw such a dreadful wound.   One of the poor beaters was mauled, though not severely—only a rip across the thigh about four inches long, but rather deep— he will soon be well again.   Pig-sticking is certainly a very fine sport, and, in my opinion, Dubka is a sort of everything to Baroda.   The best thing the Rajah ever did, I should think, is allowing us to hunt there ; at least, I have not enjoyed anything so much since I have been in India.   It has quite put a stop to all my shooting.   I have now seen a little fox-hunting and a little hog-hunting, and, in my humble opinion, the fox gives the best amusement, and the hog the best sport; but I prefer the society of a hunt in England, and if I had my choice, I would rather ride with you and Charlie to see the hounds throw off at home, than go after the largest boar that ever was born out here."

CHAPTER II.

SPORT AT BARODA—PIG AND TIGER.   1849-1851.

IN February, 1849, Johnson wrote to his brother:
" I think you will like to hear of a three days' trip
we had to Dubka, about fifteen miles from this, on
the banks of the Myr ; but first of all I must tell
you that the Rajah went there to his preserves on a
shooting expedition. Captain French, his Resident
here, and Battye, his assistant, asked me to go out
there with them ; in fact, the whole camp were
asked, but only Glasspoole and myself went. The
first day we did nothing but a little innocent snipe-
shooting. The next morning we went out with the
Rajah to see the cheetah hunting—very tame work,
but curious and interesting to see once. The deer
are much tamer in these preserves than any I have
yet seen in India. 'Of course, it is easier to account
for, as no one is allowed to shoot there. The
cheetahs are all taken on carts drawn by two

bullocks, and as soon as they are able to get within
150 or 200 yards of the deer, the hood is taken off
his eyes, and he is slipped at them. He generally
picks out the buck, does not go very fast at first, but
when he gets fairly into his stride, you never saw
such wonderful speed. You will fancy what it is,
when I tell you he will catch a black buck before
he has run 150 yards. As soon as he comes up to
him, he darts at his throat, and, with the wonderful
impetus, they roll over and over for about twenty
yards, but he never leaves go his hold, and there
they remain until some one comes up and secures
the cheetah and cuts the deer's throat. They don't
appear to have much pluck, for if they are not able
to catch the deer before he has run 300 or 400 yards,
they give in, and are brought back and put in the
cart again.

"We got back to breakfast about two p.m., and
after breakfast I told Battye I was going to look after
some pig, in what I thought was a very likely place,
and asked him to bring a spear and come too, in case
we saw anything; but he was tired, and said it was
of no use going out without having made an arrange-
ment beforehand. However, this did not stop me,
and I got hold of six beaters and went by myself,
and before we had been in the jungle ten minutes

(it was low jungle with an open space here and there in it) up started five and went into the thick part again; after beating about half an hour we started another, which came back towards me. I got a scurry for about five minutes amongst the trees and bushes, which were so thick I soon lost him. Well, coming home we were so fortunate as to come across about fourteen, going over the hills to feed. They did not see me until I came within about eighty yards of them, and then most of them cut away as soon as possible, but two of the larger ones stood and looked at me, as if they did not know what was going on. However, as soon as I got close upon them, they turned round and went away: two across a scraggy hedge (no jump) into a road, and out the other side into a sort of plain, with a quantity of low bushes every here and there. I picked out the largest I saw, and went after him for about a couple of miles. I could not get anywhere near him at first. I had no idea they went such a pace. At last I began to gain upon him, and came within about ten yards of him, when, to my horror, he disappeared in some jungle I had not seen before, and I lost him. If I had known he had been making for this covert, I would have pressed him more at first, but he dodged round the bushes so actively, I could not have killed him by myself. The ground was rough and hard, but no holes and very little jumping. He went through two thick prickly-pear hedges, which, I should have thought, would have pierced any other animal to death ; they were quite low, and I was surprised he did not jump them ; but from what I saw, I fancy they never jump anything. He went a wonderful pace, much faster than I expected ; but this was a perfectly fresh hog, which had not been hunted about by the beaters beforehand, as is generally the case. The horse, the new bay one, carried me, like the perfect darling that he is. He jumps beautifully, and is very clever at getting over rough, broken ground ; in fact, he is quite perfection.

"Now for the next day, the big go, when the Rajah turned out with all his retinue of elephants and horses: about three thousand beaters are sent to one side (a large space of jungle with the river Myr on the other) ; they surround the game and beat it all towards the Rajah (who sits on one of the elephants with a silk umbrella, eating betel-nuts), and as soon as a head of game of any description shows itself, some of his horsemen with spears and swords go after it. I was so glad when the poor deer escaped ; and once I forgot myself and halloa'd out 'hurrah' when a poor hare, with about five hundred people of every description after it, with dogs, etc., escaped unhurt, much to the disgust of the Maharajah. Battye and I sent on our horses and spears ahead, and came down on one of the elephants to the ground, where we dismounted. However, I missed Battye in the crowd, and did not see him again till the end of the day, so I got my horse and went on beyond where the Rajah was, and waited for the first hog that came by: and, sure enough, in about half an hour they began to come, and as soon as I saw one large one, with a lot of fellows after him, I gathered up the reins and followed. I don't know whether it is the natives' fault or their horses', but certainly they could not go any pace at all, and as soon as I put the steam on, I passed them like a shot, and when I got into a small open space, I went still faster, as fast as I could go, got the spear down, and gave it to him as deep as I could. As he felt the spear, he gave a grunt and turned round at me; but I was going much too fast to get damaged in any way. After this he got into a patch of jungle about a hundred yards square, and there he remained, charging everything that came near him. I rode at him again, and before I could get the spear at him, he turned round as I was passing him, and tried to rip up the horse; fortunately his lower tush caught my foot below the instep, and saved him (the horse), giving me nothing more than a bruise across the leather of the boot. He was one of the most savage beasts I ever saw ; he came across a poor little boy on foot, about fourteen or fifteen years old, knocked him down, ripped up his arm, and sent his tush in an inch and a half deep, and there he stood, with the fellow's turban in his mouth looking, at him. Afterwards I came at him again, and when I got within eight yards he turned round and charged me. Fortunately my horse made a spring and cleared him, and got off scot-free. Afterwards the other fellows killed him, which I was very glad of; but it was my hog, as I struck him first, but I can't say it was much credit, as no white faces were riding against me. Afterwards Battye and I went after another, and came up to him together, but I was nearest the hog, and was getting the spear down, when he turned sharp round, came against the horse, and sent us both spinning about twenty yards. I picked up the spear, and went to work again, but Battye had killed him before I reached him. He was a very large hog, but not so big as the first one. Thus ended the best three days' sport I have yet had in India. I came back to the huts pretty well done, with the happy prospect of a fifteen-mile ride back into camp. I got here at two in the morning, and had to turn out at four for parade."

In May, 1849, he describes an excursion after bears: "I started on the evening of the 13th April, rode out the first eight miles on a horse I got for the occasion, and went the rest of the way in a cart, arriving at Champaneer, the village I intended to stay at, at sunrise. We were delayed in the middle of the night by our guide, who, as soon as he had got us well into the middle of the wood, thought fit to run away, and it was two or three hours, after having gone in the wrong direction, that we found another. This fellow seemed inclined to bolt too, so I secured some of his clothes, and put them behind me in the cart, and we got on without any trouble. It is a beautiful country for shooting, just at the beginning of that long range of hills running down to Surat. I got on famously with the natives out there. They were very independent, and almost every one carries his matchlock, to pot the deer when they come in their way. However, I found that by treating them well, and paying them well, I became capital friends with them, and they want me to go out again after the first fall of rain, when they say I shall shoot cheetah and sambre to any amount. I shot two bears; they were very large ones—indeed, one was upwards of five feet. It is difficult to come across them, because they only come out at night to feed, and come back to their caves at daybreak, where they remain the whole day, so the only plan is to get up in the night, and be ready to receive them up at the rocks, as they come home in the morning. I was disappointed the first time, for none came; but one of the beaters, a famous fellow, always in the right place, spied one at some distance going under a great piece of rock, and after a good deal of hullabalooing and rolling down pieces of rock, out he came with a rush, making a tremendous row, something between a hoarse pig and a bull. I shot him before he had gone half-a-dozen yards, and he died instantaneously.

"The other one I got two or three days afterwards, at a village about seven miles further on. I arrived there about midnight; two bears came home just before sunrise, but went into some holes too far away to be shot at. Again the next morning I was up there, and put myself close to the hole that I thought was their favourite one. They soon came. I dropped a bullet into the largest; he began twirling round and round on his hind legs, and I thought he was done for, and shot the second barrel at the other, thinking it would be such a fine thing to have a double shot at bears, and bag them both; but to my great dismay he got up, and before I could get another gun, both of them had got under the rocks. The following morning, behind a clump of bamboos, they came out growling, and evidently remarkably sulky. I shot at one, and hit him very hard indeed, but it did not stop him. I ran after him with the second barrel, and found them both together behind a large stone. One got off, but I got the first one, as he could not go any further. I got Walker's gun, which was loaded with Eley's cartridges, and fired a couple of shots at him, but I might as well have thrown my hat at him. They won't answer at all for bears; they have such immense bone and muscle.

"Great excitement took place at the spot where we encamped in, one evening just after sunset. I was away at the top of the hill, but my washerman and two cartmen were sitting talking together, when up comes a very hungry-looking tiger, and stood and looked at them for about half a minute. All three of them were in such fright, that not one had breath enough to holloa out and drive him away; at the last they all crawled up to the top of the cart, and the beast went away without doing any damage. There

were a great many tigers at the second place I went
to; pugs in every direction. I sat out the whole of one
night to wait for them to come and drink. They all
came round me; I was in a tree about twelve feet
from the ground, but as the night was nearly pitch
dark, I was unable to see them. They made a fearful row, and appeared to smash everything that came
in their way. The noise they made was unlike anything I ever heard; a sort of peculiar gurgling in the
throat, which one could have heard a mile off. I saw
a panther one day as I was looking for bears; I ran
after him to try and get a shot, but he sneaked away.
The bears shed two of the most beautiful skins you
ever saw. I did my best to take care of them. A
curious incident happened one day. Whilst one of
the beaters was passing two or three large pieces of
rock with some holes under them, out comes a large
she bear, roaring like a bull, and makes for the first
one she sees; knocks him down, lays hold of him,
shaking and biting him very badly indeed. She was
soon shouted and pelted off, and was coming to
Glasspoole, to serve him the same, but a shot turned
her, and she did not do any more damage. They
picked the man up, who was senseless from fright and
pain, but they soon brought him round again with a
little brandy."

In April, 1850, Johnson made another expedition to the same place, and writes : " The bears apparently got such a dusting last year, that they have almost deserted the place where we used to shoot them, but the last day coming home we had a bit of excitement after one, and boned him too. He didn't at all appear to relish being disturbed so early after his nightly rovings, for he tried hard to lay hold of one or two of the beaters, and one very wisely jumped up in a tree as quickly as he could. I killed him the third shot with Walker's gun, the bullet passing through one ear and out at the other.   He was a fine bear, and I shall keep the skin and the skull.   There was bear's-grease to any extent, but the idea of saving any never entered my head, or I would have done so.   I shall try to go out again for three days at the full moon, not exactly to the same place, but ten miles further on, where a man is going to dig a hole for me, close to some water, where I am to be deposited at sunset, and he declares I shall have three or four shots."   It was here Johnson for the first time met Captain Fulljames, Commandant of the Guzerat Horse, and afterwards so intimate a friend.

A book, called " Traits and Anecdotes of Animals," was published in 1861, by Bentley & Son, to which Johnson contributed the following remarks on shooting bears: " Bears generally go in couples. On one occasion I became aware of some rocks, where bears were known to live, but there was no getting them out. Knowing that they always go out to feed at night, and return about sunrise, I went before dawn to the rocks, and had hardly taken up my position, before I saw them coming one after the other. I took a shot at the leading one, and hit him somewhere about his tail ; he was probably under the impression that his companion had bitten him on the stern, for he turned round and furiously seized him ; they both rolled over, and had a most terrible battle ; it was truly ludicrous. I have seldom known tigers or bears to charge without provocation or being wounded. I have seen and shot many bears, and only on one occasion have I seen them make an assault. It was when a party of men were going through some rocks, a bear came out suddenly, seized one of the beaters, shook him well, put him down, and escaped. Bears sometimes carry off a wonderful deal of lead. I have shot them through and through, and yet they have made their way into the jungle and escaped."

In a letter to his mother from Baroda, he describes the robberies that took place there. " The Guzeratees," he says, "are famous hands at this work ; they generally prefer boring holes through walls to any other plan ; they then grease their bodies all over, so if any one tries to catch them, they slip through their fingers like an eel." In another letter he says : " Nixon is gone away sick, and I am acting for him as Quartermaster, Paymaster, and Interpreter. I have quite enough to live upon, and don't want any more. As for making a fortune out here, I wouldn't do it if I could. In my humble opinion, a great deal too much money goes home from this country. We have taken India, and have improved its manu- factures and agriculture, but this is no reason why the value of the whole of the produce should go to England, which it does in great measure, while the poorer clases out here have scarcely bread to put in their mouths. What I mean is, that the value of the productions of this country should be spent in it, and not go further."

His time at Baroda was by no means all spent in sport, much as he loved it. He worked very hard at the languages, and passed the Interpreter's examin- ation in Hindustani and in Mahratti. In January, 1850, he wrote from Bombay to his mother of the latter examination : " I see by this morning's paper that my name is at the top of the list, so I must have made the best examination of the lot, which is

more than I expected." There was no one in the
station who had passed in Mahratti, or indeed knew
anything about it; and this advantage made him
eligible for staff appointments. Lord Falkland,
who had for some time promised to help him,
appointed him acting adjutant of the Southern
Mahratta Horse, stationed at Belgaum, with a
promise that if he remained steady he should gain
advancement.

He left Baroda in the autumn of 1850 for Belgaum,
where he was stationed about six months. He was
very happy there, and enjoyed the climate, place,
and society as well as the sport, of which there was
a good deal. He had some excellent pig-sticking,
and shot some panthers. In May, 1851, Lord Falkland appointed him to the adjutancy of the Guzerat
Horse, stationed at Ahmadabad, of which Captain
Fulljames was Commandant.

He left Belgaum for Bombay to take up this
appointment in May, and did the 303 miles in seven
days and a half, the quickest march he had done as yet.
He rode on ponies by day and travelled in bullock-
carts at night. Writing to his brother in July, 1851,
from Ahmadabad, he says: "I don't know what to
think of this place. One seldom likes a place till one is
settled, and I have a wretched hole to live in, as bad a

situation as could be—the city wall, which is about as high as the roof, running close in front of it on the west, and thereby keeping off every bit of the only good wind we have. But this will not last very long, as I hope soon to get something settled about the bit of ground I want on the opposite side of the river, and then I can begin my own house. From inquiries I have made, it will be much less expensive than I anticipated. I should say it will be nearer 1500 than 2000 rupees ; but even if it cost 2500 rupees I should be a gainer rather than a loser, besides the comfort of living in one's own house and garden, instead of being in the middle of a dirty city.   I like what I have seen of Captain and Mrs. Fulljames: he is a thorough straightforward gentleman and a first-rate soldier, and every one is very fond of Mrs. Fulljames."

They did not, however, remain much longer at Ahmadabad, for in September, 1851, he wrote to his mother: "We have lost our old Commandant, Captain Fulljames, much to the regret of every one, as he had been with the regiment about ten years, and was much beloved ; there is not a man in the corps who won't regret him. He goes to take up a Political Agency in the country north of Baroda."   His successor was Captain Leeson. Mrs. Leeson was a great rider across country, and Johnson often lent her his favourite "Arab's Choice." "It is worth five rupees of any one's money," he said, "to see the way she puts him along: it is quite magnificent."

CHAPTER III.

AHMADABAD—LARGE GAME SHOOTING, PIG-STICKING. 1851–1854.

THE city of Ahmadabad stands on the river Sambermutta. It contains most splendid mosques and tombs of the kings of Guzerat, and is noted for the elaborate beauty of the carving on many of the old houses, as well as on the mosques and tombs. There are magnificent trees on each side of the broad road which connects the city with the cantonment. It was taken by the British in 1817, and has gone on steadily increasing in importance ever since.

The house which Johnson built for himself was situated on the bank of the river, looking across to the city; it consisted of dining-room, bedroom, and office, with excellent stables, well, and gardens. "You will be surprised," he wrote, "when I tell you I can get fifty square feet of masonry, bricks and all, finished for five shillings. All the houses here are built of old bricks which abound in every direction—they are found close under the surface of the ground—the whole place appears to be one mass of ruins. The stables are built after a plan of my own, and are very much approved by all who have seen them."

In October, 1851, he wrote to his brother: "I have lots of employment now, having twelve years of official correspondence to read up about the Guzerat Horse, and they are going to make me a magistrate, so I must read up Guzeratti for my magisterial business. What with the new house and garden, the new flute and the magisterial duties, I hope to keep myself out of mischief for the next few years. There's a report that the 6th are to go to Loheia to fight the Arabs, and catch the man who murdered Captain Milne the other day near Aden. If a native regiment, it would probably be the 6th, but I doubt if Government would send a large body of troops on such a wild-goose chase as this would be. I believe the Loheia people are perfectly defenceless, and can only run away; but if they go across the desert and we have to follow them, it would be a great bore." Later he writes : "There is a rumour just arrived that the Governor and Commandant have just come down from the hills post-haste, to send off troops to the Cape. This interests me particularly, because if they send the 6th I shall be very happy to go with them.   I should much prefer going to fight the Hottentots at the Cape, to running after Arabs and living upon coffee at Mocha."

In February, 1852, Billy went to live in his new house (which he had sold, after commencing it, to a Parsee, who finished it for him), and here he lived with his friend Nicholson.   He writes: "I am as happy and comfortable as I can be, with such nice people as the Leesons, Babingtons, Seward and Whitehill are. I often go over after an evening ride, and we all dine together, and have a cheroot at the top of the house; much jollier than dining at home, which I have a great aversion to.   However, I take good care not to go unless I'm asked, because hospitality is carried to such an extent in this country, that a youngster walks into a good-natured man's house, and gets a footing there, and does whatever he likes, until the good-natured man votes him a bore, but does not know how to get rid of him; and this is how the good-natured man gets into debt, because it appears a natural consequence that every one who comes to see you must be in a state of thirst, and must have a bottle of soda-water and brandy, and then a cheroot or two, as a matter of course, to finish off with.   I send a picture of my estate.   You must understand that the bed of the river is a quarter of a mile broad, but the stream, except in the monsoon, is only about forty or fifty yards, and in many places quite shallow. The bank on which our house stands is a good height above the river, so we are well open to the breeze."

Besides the friends above named, with whom he lived at Ahmadabad, much as if they were one large family, there were Harington Bulkley, and Gordon Cumming, brother of the celebrated lion-hunter, both very keen sportsmen, and to both of whom Johnson was greatly attached. They were employed in the Revenue Survey Department in Guzerat. Poor Bulkley lost his life in consequence of a wound from a tiger, which caused an abscess, from which, after undergoing an operation some years later, he died. "Billy" described this adventure in a letter to his mother from Poona: "My friend Bulkley has been boned by a tiger, and a good deal mouthed. He is up here now on sick certificate; and though his back and shoulder are a good deal lacerated, he is in just as good spirits as ever, and being old friends, we are a good deal together. The tiger, without being wounded, charged him out of some bushes, and Bulkley, having the hundred yards sight up, missed it coming on. It bowled him over and caught him in his mouth by the shoulder, shook him, dragged him down the ravine, and then let him go. The wound is awfully poisonous always, and takes a long time to heal."

With Harington Bulkley and Gordon Cumming Billy had many an expedition after large game. It was about this time that he met with an accident with a panther. "I believe," he wrote, "there is not a more treacherous or dangerous animal than a panther, —many more accidents happen with panthers than with tigers in India. On one occasion we had wounded the mother of some cubs, and we went after her with great caution—well armed with guns, spears, and shields, all covering the puggee or tracker, who went close in front of us. She was waiting, and charged straight on us from behind the root of a tree. I jumped on one side, gave her a shot as she went past, and hit her in the neck. She charged on from one man to another, each having a shot or cut at her with his sword. I never saw such a game brute in my life, as she continued to charge from one to the other, until she had no breath left in her body. We took the cubs home, and I brought one up, and a voracious little savage he proved: he used to hunt the goats and poultry, and finished up by devouring part of a pair of flannel pants and a leather razor-case. I had observed the brute getting poorly, and administered two grains of tartar emetic, and two of calomel, which caused him to vomit up the articles. There was once marked down for me in a small patch of bushes a large panther which I knew to be very severely wounded, and I thought disabled. I took my rifle —a handy, double-barrelled Lancaster—and walked towards the bushes. When I was within forty yards, he came out at me so quickly that I had but just time to put up my rifle, and fire both barrels as quick as I could. Most fortunately one bullet entered just above the left eye, and came out behind the ear, somewhat confusing him, but not in the least checking his speed. He knocked me over, and bit and clawed me severely. Some of my men of the Guzerat Irregular Horse behaved very well, and, attacking him, drove him off me with their swords and carbines ; we killed him at last, but I had a very narrow escape."*

The panther tore him all down his leg, and he used to describe how his native servant rubbed the wounds with brandy, giving him terrible pain. He alludes to this in a letter to his mother: "You seem to have been in a great state of alarm about my accident, which I am sorry for. I think I told you I was nearly all right, and there was no cause to be anxious about it, although it was lucky it was no worse ; and in one

* This anecdote was published in "Traits and Anecdotes of Animals."

respect I dare say it is a good thing, as now, perhaps, it will be a warning to take better protection next time.   Young Barton, of the Artillery, has been wounded much in the same way, but he was more mauled than I was; the tiger took him up and shook him, and knocked his head against the rocks; but he is a tough little chap, and is all right again now. Graham, who was close to him at the time, fell off the same rock down below without a gun, and had the satisfaction of looking on, expecting his turn would come next, and as soon as the brute caught his eye he came at him, but luckily missed him."

In September, 1852, "Billy" wrote to his brother, describing the Ahmadabad races: "My little horse, The Arab's Choice, has been doing wonders, and has proved himself the best horse in Guzerat.   I put him in four of the best races, and he won them all, the last with the greatest ease in the world.   I always knew he was a good, game little nag, but never the least expected he was coming out in this way.   Lots of chaps want to get hold of him, but I have refused three thousand rupees for him.   He has won me eight hundred rupees by stakes and entrances, and I won between six and seven hundred rupees more, in backing my own opinion.   The horse cost me nine hundred rupees, so, you see, he has won me more than his price. What the horse's pedigree is, I don't know, but he certainly must have some first-rate lasting blood in him, for he was not the least distressed, although, as far as speed goes, for a short distance, some of his races were very close indeed. He's a well-made horse, and his style of galloping beautiful, but the great perfection in his build is, he has such fine, large, flat legs between the knee and fetlock—a part where Arabs almost invariably break down. A native always rides for me, an old man; but more about him next time, as now I must tell you about the grand event, the steeplechase, which, of course, I rode myself. The distance was about two miles and a half; two brooks; six hurdles; two high, broad hedges, and a brick wall; all artificial except one brook. The hedges were the only big jumps in the race. The first brook I led over with another man, and raced up to the first hurdle, and I landed safe the other side, just as his head came in contact with the ground. He was the only man I was afraid of, and, after this, I had it all my own way, and won in a walk. The Arab jumped everything beautifully, and was very much admired. But the unlucky part of the race is to come. On going to scales, I found that during the race two saddle-cloths had got out from under the saddle without my knowing anything

about it at the time, and I was under weight by about
half a pound.   It was so near, that I actually got the
weight off the ground, but could not weigh it down ;
and the stewards were obliged to give it against me ;
so the second horse got the stakes, and I and the
Arab the honour of coming in first.   It was a loss to
me of £30, which is a consideration at any time,
but I was more sorry, on account of the men who
had backed the horse. I even saddled him myself, and did not think it possible anything could
escape, but at each jump they must by degrees
have worked themselves out, and then flew away
behind."

About the same time he wrote: "I hate this
country quite as much as ever, and rather more, if
possible.   I can't make a residence out of England.
I want to see some healthy-looking English faces
again ; I feel as if even that would do me good.
We are all of us on a wild-goose chase after some
murderers, about eighty or a hundred miles off, and
we are going to try and put some salt on their tails ;
but I am afraid they are quite sure to get news of
our whereabouts, and bolt before we get near them.
We shall get a lot of snipe, and perhaps have a run
after a pig."   He writes later : "We contrived to get
three days' hunting, and killed five pig. The first

run was the only good one, and I think was the best I ever have seen, and certainly the longest, for I suppose from the place we found to the place where the pig died, could not have been less than five miles, and over a very excellent country, which made it all the better fun, and we were all close up at the first spear, which was taken by one Barton, who thoroughly deserved it, for he rides magnificently. I never saw a man ride a pig so perfectly as he does. He belongs to the Artillery, rather short and stoutly made, and rides an Arab galloway, one of the cleverest animals I suppose that ever was foaled. It is a treat to see a man go across country in the way he does."

In March, 1853, Billy was appointed second in command, during the absence of his friend Nicholson, who held that post, and with whom he lived. He was also acting adjutant. Early in the month he had a few days' leave for shooting, and wrote to his mother: "Here I am at a place called Rehma Tursung, not far from the Myr River, under some mango trees, and sitting on my bed in a very small tent, ten feet by eight, and the sun just getting up— three camels and horses of sorts, and a waterman's bullock picketed close by. This is such a nice place, nothing but mango trees and large rocks, and no end of a wild country all round. It seems quite a relief after Ahmadabad, and I could stop here with pleasure a couple of months. The men are gone down to the rocks in the river to-day, and I hope will be able to find the whereabouts of a tiger, or a panther ; if not, I shall go and beat the ravine in that direction, and they say I am pretty sure to see something. You have no idea how careful I've become since my accident last year. We had a very good run at Warwal, one of the best I have ever seen in India, and lots of difficulties. I met with an accident, as usual, for I got up to the boar first, having ridden him pretty close the whole way, but only touched his back ; and as I prefer a short spear, the head went into the ground, and the butt-end just caught me on the side above the liver. It was very severe, and I had to get off and lie under a tree, but I have felt no ill effects since."

In May, 1853, he wrote to his sister : "I think I told you I was going after large game as soon as Leeson returned. I shot a large tigress, which they said had killed a couple of men; but this I can't answer for. We had great excitement after an enormous bear one day. I got him marked down beautifully, but he broke in rather a difficult place to get a clear shot at him, and it was some time before I could get hold of my second rifle (such a beauty! one of Leeson's—a Westley Richards, about eleven bore). He charged at the third shot, and when he had got away about fifty yards, came grunting and barking as hard as he could, straight at me. I thought I was most likely in for it again, as I was nearest the brute. I did not know whether to cut or stand, for I had only one barrel loaded, but fortunately stood where I was, and when he got within about twenty yards, let drive, and caught him somewhere between the neck and shoulders, and he turned instanter. Didn't my heart beat! If I had looked round I should have bolted, for all the niggers sang out to me to get up a tree; but luckily I did not hear them, as there could not possibly have been time."

He suffered very much from fever at Ahmadabad in the summer of 1853, and applied for leave to go to Khandalah or Mahableshwur; but a short trip he took to Cambay did him much good, and he did not go to Mahableshwur until the end of the year, returning by way of Poona.

The story of these years of his life may well end with two extracts from letters written by his intimate friends General Harpur and Dr. Greenhow. General Harpur writes: "Poor Jansing! (I feel I must call him by the old familiar name) he was such a plucky, resolute fellow.   To us in the regiment he was known as a good, steady, hardworking, zealous soldier,* very fearless and determined, regardless of difficulties.   He would go through and carry out anything he took in hand.   He was a courageous and keen sportsman, especially in pursuit of large game, and a very reliable man to have by one in time of danger and need."   Dr. Greenhow writes : " He was very keen on sport, and used to be intensely excited when a pig was afoot, riding hard to get the first spear, which he often succeeded in doing. Then his marshalling the long line of coolies was a sight to see, explaining as he did to each man what was expected of him, and ending with promises of ' backsheesh ' if they drove out the pig success-fully."

It is not surprising that a soldier so plucky and resolute was longing for active service in the field. India was at this time perfectly quiet, and it was just now that the war with Russia broke out.   Hear-ing that officers were wanted for service with the

---

* The following note is from the Regimental Order-book at Ahmada-bad, on Captain Fulljames giving over the command of the Guzerat Horse to Captain Leeson : " Ahmadabad, 9th August, 1851.   To Lieutenant and Adjutant Johnson the Commanding Officer's best thanks are due, for the zeal and service he has performed during the time he has been with the regiment. (Signed) GEORGE FULLJAMES, Commanding Guzerat Irregular Horse."

Bashi Bozouks, he obtained six months' leave from India on private affairs, intending when he had seen his friends in England to apply at the India House for service in Turkey. On June 19th, 1854, he wrote from Tannah, near Bombay, as follows to his mother: " You know I have been expecting an answer to my application for leave, and at Ahmadabad on the 3rd inst. I found myself in orders for a furlough for six months on private affairs. I settled everything as quick as I could ; gave over The Arab's Choice to the care of one of my native officers, to be particularly taken care of, as this is the only thing I have any great affection for, and left the next day for Surat, with a few boxes and one servant, on three camels, pushing on night and day in hopes of catching the last steamer from Surat. I accomplished the 155 miles in less than four days, a march which I am sure poor old Charlie Napier could not have grumbled at, and you may fancy what a severe trial it was to find the steamer had started the day before, but had been obliged to put back, having been nearly lost trying to get over the bar. This occasioned me another trip of twelve miles to try and get aboard of her, but the boatmen said they could not manage it with the wind against them. Well, I was obliged to come back to Surat, and the next day started overland to

Bombay. A letter reached me at Surat from the Adjutant-General, saying my leave had been granted, subject to the Government of India's decision, whether or not I should be entitled to receive pay and to retain my appointment in the Guzerat Horse during my absence. I shall go on to-morrow to Bombay, and try to learn if any answer has been received from the Government of Bengal, and if I can retain the appointment; and if so, I shall start by to-morrow's steamer. But I don't like to leave India with the chance of losing my appointment in the Guzerat Horse, which, though a badly paid one, is one of the most gentlemanly we have on this side of India; and having served in this line more than four years, I have no intention of giving it up if I can possibly help it.

"I have never had such a march in my life as this one. I don't know what I have lived upon. The only things I have enjoyed have been some shrimps now and then, some English bottled beer, and some tea; but whatever I *have* lived upon, I am remarkably well, and fit for anything. It is very odd, but the rougher the life, the better I am in health, and, except last night, I have not had a night's rest in bed since I was at Surat, on the 10th. On the trip down, my camel shut up once in the middle of a plain, and would not go on, on any terms, and so I had to pad it a short way, which, with the thermometer at 120°, wasn't very nice. At another place, Damaun, they stole my big copper washing-basin, which was a considerable loss, and ever since I have had nothing to bathe in but the milk-jug! You never saw such a country or such roads. There is no made road at all, except what the carts have made for themselves—big ruts, and so awfully uneven in depth, that I was as near as possible capsized lots of times; and besides this, there are between forty and fifty rivers between this and Surat, and not a single bridge, and no boat at all, so we could not cross them till the tide had run out. I never had such a rough march in my life; and the people are so dirty, and everything full of bugs, so I have been nearly devoured.

"Yesterday the boatmen amused me by flinging away all the water, because I had taken some out to drink, thereby offending their religious prejudices, as they thought; but it was a mistake, as I had not touched the water. I had a beautiful cut at them afterwards, on finding that they ate fish, which in their caste is strictly forbidden. If I don't get my leave settled to-day, I must remain another month; at any rate, I am thinking of going to Poona, and I would then call upon Lord Elphinstone. I have

E

brought down the skins, no end of yellow pepper, a Manilla dress, and the big tiger's skull, all in a long box, to be sent round the Cape, in case I don't come myself overland." He finished this letter at Bombay, June 20th: "Been to the Adjutant-General, but the headquarters are at Poona, and I have no answer to the application made to Bengal, so I can't come by this mail, at any rate."

CHAPTER IV.

INKERMAN. 1854.

THE various delays recounted in the preceding letter prevented a visit to England. Johnson could only go straight from Bombay to Varna, intending to join the Bashi Bozouks. On his arrival, however, at Varna he found they had been disbanded. He therefore volunteered his services to Lord Raglan, who attached him to Her Majesty's 20th Foot—"the Fighting 20th"—and he was present at the embarkation of the troops at Varna and subsequent landing at Eupatoria. On his arrival in the Crimea he wrote :—

> "Crimea. Landing Place (no name to it),
> "September 18, 1854.

"MY DEAREST MOTHER,

"You mustn't be alarmed at this paper, but as we have to carry all our goods and chattels on our back, I haven't much room for pen and ink, which

I have been obliged to borrow. You will be glad to hear that I have been so fortunate as to get attached to the 20th Queen's. I had great difficulty about it, having no introductions. But I knew Captain Methven, of the *Colombo*, with the 20th on board, and he very kindly, when we arrived off the Crimea, sent his boat to take me off the *Sovereign*, and gave me a passage. The next morning we went to the *Caradoc*, the boat Lord Raglan was on, and tried to get an interview. His staff were most polite and palavering, but at the same time told me I had very little chance of being attached to the Army in any way; and as his lord-ship was very busy with lots of people, I could not possibly see him. This was all I could get from them. However, fortunately, just as I was going away, who should come out of the cabin but Lord Raglan him-self, and he asked if I was the man from India. I told him what I wanted, and he did not seem to make much difficulty about it, and asked me what I would like to be attached to; and as I was then on board the *Colombo* with the 20th, I said I should like to be with them, for it is a particularly nice regiment; and he said I might be attached to the 20th, on condition Colonel Horn, the Commandant, had no objection. I never felt much more grateful for anything in my life; thanked him very much for his kindness, and

came away, and got put in orders the same day. I
never saw such a nice set of fellows as the 20th are ;
and I am now-sitting in the Light Company tent
writing this on a shako, and living with Lieutenants
Leet and MacNeill, two Irishmen of the Light
Company, in a little bell tent. Upon my word, after
a life in India, I don't think anything of roughing
it here.

"We have met with no opposition to our landing
here in the Crimea, which is most unexpected and
fortunate. I must soon pull up. I have no idea how
this will go, but I have no doubt it will go somehow.
We are all ordered to strike our tents directly, and
move on to-morrow. We are to carry no tents on
with us, and have to take everything we want on our
backs. Such a night it was!—the first we landed. No
tents, and wind and rain to any extent, and nothing
but the wet sand to lie on. I shall not forget that
night for some time. We are all pretty well here.
This appears a beautiful climate, and we have all an
unfortunate appetite for rations—salt beef and bis-
cuits and rum, and not much of that. We are close
down to the sea, within ten yards of it, and I had a
dip this morning, but I am rather afraid of bathing,
as I got fever twice from it in India ; but there is no
other means of washing here. We have bought a

pony between us three for £5, so we shall not have so much to carry on our backs. How I hope you are all right at Enborne, and how I long to hear from you! but all my letters will be at Constantinople. We march to-morrow morning, and I hope shall make short work of it into Sebastopol. I wrote by the last mail, but they told us too late, after the steamer had gone, so I tore the letter up. I should have tried to get into a cavalry regiment, but not being able to mount myself, should have had very little chance. I am looking forward with great pleasure to a gallop across country with Lucy and Charlie."

Johnson was present at the engagements of the Alma and Balaclava, and was in the trenches before Sebastopol, but it was at the battle of Inkerman that the 20th Regiment, to which he was attached, so signally distinguished itself. That regiment had a very high prestige. Kinglake writes of it:—" The 20th Regiment, with its strength of only three hundred and forty, and armed with the small-bore musket, was yet of so high a quality that it had justly been looked to as a force which might govern the crisis in any fight undertaken for the defence of the English position. The Duke of Wellington once called the 20th the most distinguished regiment in the service, and proceeded to justify praise, which at first seemed invidious, by saying it had won all its great store of fame with one battalion. It now has two." *

The battle of Inkerman began in darkness and mist at five o'clock in the morning of Sunday, the 5th of November, 1854. There is perhaps no history of any other battle in which such great numbers fought on so small a battlefield, and there are few battles which have been so sharply contested, or in which courage and endurance were so conspicuous. "The conduct of the English," writes Lieutenant-Colonel Adye, "was immortal. Though enfeebled by previous fatigue and constant night-watches, and by exposure to wet and wretchedness, on the day of trial eight thousand men resolutely maintained themselves against successive columns of attack of vastly superior numbers, and at last, when almost overpowered, they found an ever-ready and gallant ally at hand to save them in their hour of need." It was stated by Lord Raglan that he must have been attacked by at least fifty thousand men. Kinglake tells the story of the 20th Regiment's share in "governing the crisis" of the fight. "There were," he says, "near Cathcart, dispersed in the brushwood, some men who, though busied like the

* "Invasion of the Crimea," vol. v. p. 211.

rest of his troops in pursuit, could yet be reached by his orders.   They were only fifty in number, but they belonged to the 20th, a regiment of historic renown, which is famous for imparting its aggregate quality to the individual soldier. . . . Cathcart gathered together these fifty men, and with these formed rudely in line, undertook to move up against the overhanging body, some seven or eight hundred men, which stood on the crest above him.   In ascending to make their attack, these few 20th men were obstructed, and, besides, more or less thrown asunder by the varying abruptness of their activity ; but if aggregate strength was thus neutralized, the individual soldier toiled on with a determination all his own, and the twenty or thirty soldiers who formed the right of the line, had not long been climbing the steep, when they emerged all at once from below, into the close presence of the enemy.   Then, panting after their effort, they sprang at the left of the column directly confronting them, and the Russians, there exposed to the onset, began to break and give way, without awaiting the thrust of the bayonet.   Here, then, and in several places, the Russians allowed some strong wilful assailant to tear his way in through their ranks, and every intruder into their hostile mass fought hard, as may be supposed, for life no less than for victory, using sometimes the point of the bayonet, sometimes the butt-end of the bayonet, sometimes a ready fragment of rock. The disproportion of numbers was overwhelming, and one must infer, though no witnesses speak, that of the brave men who thus engulfed themselves bodily in the depths of the column, a large proportion fell slain.

"The strain that had been pressing so long upon General Pennefather's slender resources was now in some measure lightened, by the accession of Brigadier-General Goldie, with a wing of the 20th Regiment, counting 180 men under Colonel Horn, and the approach of the 57th, nearly 200 strong, under Captain Edward Stanley. Lord Raglan ordered an aide-de-camp, Captain Somerset Calthorpe, to bring forward the wing of the 20th and take it at once to General Pennefather. This was speedily done after moving up the Home ridge by ground on the right of the post road. Colonel (now Sir Frederick) Horn, with his men of the 20th, then came under fire, and he at once deployed into line, then began to move down the slope. The state of the atmosphere had by this time changed, and was clear enough to disclose a massive body of Russians pressing up through the brushwood at a distance of about a hundred yards. The men of the

20th delivered their fire, and manifesting their presence to the enemy's gunners on Shell Hill, drew upon them a shower of artillery missiles. Whilst still a good way off from the column, they understood that they were ordered to charge. They briskly worked their way forward under a powerful fire of both artillery and small arms, which was continually lessening their scanty numbers, but the obstacles of rugged ground and thick brushwood precluded them from executing what an Englishman means by a charge. Thus circumstanced, they advanced firing. Presently they found that the enemy, whilst directly confronting them with his masses, was also overlapping their line on each of its flanks, and that there was obvious room for question as to what, in such case, they should do, but in the absence of any directions proceeding from higher authority, it was judged that their right course must still be 'to force the enemy back down the hill,' and therefore fight on to the utmost against the troops straight in their front. Then ensued a combat, maintained for some time by an industrious use of the firelock, and Colonel Horn's people at length had so nearly exhausted their cartridges as to be driven to the expedient of taking ammunition from the pouches of the dead.

"But a change of temper came on, and at the thought of the bayonet, these men of the 20th seemed all to have but one will. Despite the hostile masses on their flanks, they were glowing with that sense of power, which is scarce other than power itself. To men of their corps had been committed the charge of a sacred, historic tradition, and if they were to use the enchantment, they must not endure that in their time the spell should be broken. The air was rent by a sound which, unless they be men of the initiated regiment, men speak of as 'strange and unearthly.' After nearly a century from the day when their cry became famous, and forty years from the time when it last sounded in battle, these men of the 20th had once more delivered their old 'Minden yell.' * Disregarding alike the force on their right and the force on their left, they sprang at the mass in their front, and drove it down the hillside. Following the post road, they passed over the barrier, and descended some hundreds of yards into the Quarry Ravine; but by that time they were in a dispersed state. Lieutenant Vaughan chanced to be with the foremost of the pursuing soldiery, and he found himself in command of about a score of men,

---

* It was of course by steady practice in the regiment that the art and mystery of the "Minden yell" had been faithfully preserved.

belonging partly to his own regiment (the 20th), but partly also the Guards and regiments of the 2nd Division. With the aid of a volunteer officer, Lieutenant Johnson, of the Indian Irregular Cavalry, he formed up his men across the road, and moved steadily forward, pushing always before him the enemy's disordered troops. He was approaching the part of the Quarry Ravine where it makes a sudden bend in its course, when, on looking towards the crest straight before him, he saw a Russian light battery brought rapidly on to its edge, and presently he and his men were under its plunging fire. Choosing out a few of the Guards and other men armed with a rifle, he bade them disregard altogether the enemy's infantry, sight the pieces from 300 yards, and steadily shoot at the battery. He was so well obeyed by his marksmen (they knelt down and took aim with studious, deliberate care), that the battery, after firing another round, limbered up and made off in great haste. It was only on the approach of fresh columns that the now scattered fragments of Horn's victorious soldiery, and with them Vaughan's little band, began to fall back from the advanced ground they had reached in the eagerness and heat of pursuit. Colonel Horn's wing of the 20th was never forced back to the crestwork ; sometimes losing, sometimes gaining ground, it remained fighting out in the front. Thus against the whole weight of the forces attacking the right of Home ridge, our people made good the defence, with less than four hundred men."

Describing a later period of the battle, Kinglake goes on : "Amongst the accession on the right of our line was a score of men under Vaughan [with whom was Lieutenant Johnson], chiefly men of the 20th and Guardsmen, whom we saw doing venturesome service in an earlier stage of the battle. From time to time, after retreating a little way, Vaughan caused the men with him to turn and show front, and there being a few among them who had some cartridges left, he was able to vex the assailants with occasional shots. With the right of the battalion, meanwhile, all seemed to be going ill. There, despite all the vehement efforts of the French officers, numbers not only turned and broke in disorder, but fell back so heavily upon the friendly line of the English as to burst their way through it. This occurred at the part of the line where Vaughan had drawn up the small thread of soldiers under him. Yet even in this, the most disorderly part of Vaissier's battalion, there were some that refused to yield. A young French officer hoisted his cap upon the point of his uplifted sword and ran out several paces to the front, an English officer * sprang forward and stood by his side ; another and another darted out to the same exposed spot, and there the four remained steadfast, provoking a great flight of musket balls without once being struck." †

In a letter to his mother, Johnson bears out Kinglake's description of the battle, and the part he played in it.

" November 7th, 1854.   Above Sebastopol.

" It will be safe to write at any rate, for should you hear of this business, without a list of casualties, you will be deeply anxious about me.   We had such a go on the 5th ; Alma was a joke to it, as far as the Russian loss was concerned, and our own was very severe, although I hope not half as much as Alma. The 20th, I am glad to say, were in the thick of it, so we have had our share, anyhow, as yet.   The fighting was most desperate ; we went into action with about 300 or 400 men (not so many, I think) and 18 officers.   We have had one officer killed (poor Dowling, a great friend of mine), and seven wounded, and about 170 men killed and wounded.   Our

* See letter from W. T. J. below.
† Kinglake's " Crimea," vol. v. p. 307.

general, poor Cathcart, was killed ; both our brigadiers wounded (one dead since). Sir George Brown wounded ; in fact, we lost some of our best men yesterday, men we can't spare. Old Cathcart I used to love, like every one else. He got too far down the hill. He was with a lot of the 20th and the Guards, and went after the fellows too far, where there was hard fighting going on to the left and above. There were no end of Russians, columns after columns, and the cavalry all ready below to finish the business when their swarms of infantry had carried the heights. However, part of our division, the Guards, and a few of the 2nd Division, held the ground until the French came up; and then *didn't* we give it them : French and ourselves all mixed up together ! I know a French officer and myself* were the two first ahead. I was sure it was all right when we began to advance, but before that we had been out of ammunition ; and although holding the ground as tight as we could, we were driven to the very tops of the heights, when like a perfect godsend the French came to our assistance, and the firing was so thick then, and the Russians had gained such confidence, that it was even several minutes before we could make an impression

* These are doubtless the French and English officers mentioned by Kinglake above.

on them again. I did not get near enough to the Russians to have a cut at one, but I pelted some with big pieces of stones.* The whizzing of balls and grape was something awful, and I fully expected to be shot every minute. Our colonel, major, and adjutant, our only mounted officers, all had their horses killed. Lots of fellows were tumbling over close to me, and a mounted officer could not live in it for five minutes. I thank God, and so must you all, that I am out of it with whole bones, for I had several shaves, and one ball came through my trousers just below the knee, and another through my coat on the left side. I am glad I have been in a general action at last, and I wasn't as much excited as I expected, and I can fight as well as any one, for I was well in front; and the Colonel of the 20th, Colonel Horn, after he saw me safe afterwards, shook me by the hand and said, 'Your name shall go to India for this; at least, it shall if I have anything to do with it.' Very flattering I thought it, though I don't know that I deserve it particularly, except that I did some good, and made the fellows fight as well

---

* Kinglake speaks of the fighting with stones : " With some of the Grenadiers on the right, ammunition began to fail, and a few of their immediate adversaries were feeling the same want, for the combatants on each side at this spot, began to hurl against one another some of the loose pieces of rock which strewed the ground."—Vol. v. p. 322.

as I could. Both the fellows in my tent are wounded, and I have not time for any more. The action began at daylight, and they tried to surprise us, and were up to our tents almost before we knew where they were; but they have met with awful loss. I went over the field of battle yesterday with a bottle of water, to give any fellows I found wounded. I think the Russians must have lost four or five to every one of ours. I had no idea they would fight so well; I expect they were well crammed with liquor. Duke Constantine was commanding in person."

Colonel Horn kept his word. He reported the gallant conduct of the young Lieutenant of Indian Horse to the India House, and the Directors forwarded his despatch, with strong approval, to the Governor-General, who emphasized his satisfaction in the most signal manner; he published it to the army in India :—

"The Right Honourable the Governor in Council has much satisfaction in publishing to the army the following letter from Brigadier F. Horn, commanding the 1st Brigade, 4th Division, of the Army of the Crimea, dated Camp at Sebastopol, to the Chairman of the Honourable Court of Directors.

F

"Camp near Sebastopol, Nov. 18th, 1854.

" SIR,

"I trust you will kindly pardon the liberty I take as an utter stranger, in thus addressing you, as I feel it would be an act of injustice on my part to allow the departure of Lieutenant Johnson of the 6th Bombay Native Infantry, and Irregular Cavalry, who has for upwards of two months been attached to the 20th Regiment, by Lord Raglan's order, without bearing testimony to his gallant behaviour at the recent terrific action of Inkerman, which victory is allowed even to have eclipsed that of the Alma. I beg therefore to state that in the early part of the action of the 5th November the 20th, then under my command, had the misfortune to lose ten officers, including one killed, and the 4th Division to which it belonged also lost the general (the Honourable Sir George Cathcart) and two brigadiers, which called me, as next in seniority, to command the division. I cannot, therefore, speak in terms of sufficient praise of the cool and determined bravery, combined with intelligence, of Mr. Johnson on the occasion, when the regiment had, as described, lost so many of its members. His presence on the battlefield was singularly useful in cheering and directing the men, and I cannot but see in him the promise of a most efficient and valuable officer to the service to which he belongs; and he now leaves the Crimea and his companions in arms of the 20th Regiment, to the universal regret of the latter, and in consequence of his furlough having nearly expired.

> "I have the honour to remain, etc.,
>
> "FREDERICK HORN,
>
> "Col. and Lieut.-Col. and Actg. Brig.-Gen.,
> 1st Brigade, 4th Div.

" To Major Oliphant, Chairman to the Hon.
Court of Directors, East India Company."

APPENDIX TO CHAPTER IV.

LETTERS AND DESPATCHES RELATING TO THE CRIMEAN CAMPAIGN.

Brigadier-General Horn to Lieutenant W. T. Johnson.

> Camp before Sevastopol,
> 24th January, 1855.

MY DEAR JOHNSON,

I should have replied to your letter of 24th December long since, but for the fact of my having waited for the decision of the Field-Marshal, on a point in reference to myself. After I had transmitted the list of those who were entitled to the honorary distinction of medals and clasps belonging to the 20th, it struck me that no man in the regiment had a better right to such marks of distinction than yourself. I therefore addressed Lord Raglan on the subject, and though I have as yet received no answer to my application, I trust there is but little doubt that you will eventually obtain a Crimean medal and two clasps for your services in the field at the battles of Alma and Inkerman. Please, therefore, inform me whether they shall be sent to the India House for transmission to you in India, or where else you would like them sent, for as a British officer, you are, as I said before, clearly entitled to them. I have now to thank you for the handsome and timely present of the fur coat ; it is not only handsome but useful in the extreme. The weather has been fearful. It snowed for about three days almost incessantly, and many poor fellows were frozen to death, and lost in the snow-drifts, including a Captain of the 9th Regiment. The sufferings of our poor soldiers have been much underrated, even in the accounts given by the *Times* paper ; and the exertions of the generous-hearted people of England have in a measure been abortive, from the difficulty, nay, almost impossibility of getting up from Balaklava the tons weight of warm clothing sent out for our poor soldiers. Many of our wounded have died at Scutari of hospital gangrene, amongst them poor Major Sharpe. Butler has just returned to camp. The siege operations have nearly stopped for the present, but the duty in the trenches, I need hardly say, is more severe than ever on account of the weather. I shall be glad to hear from you, and meanwhile

Believe me, yours truly,

FRED. HORN.

II.

Major-General Yorke to Lieut.-General Sir Henry Somerset, K.C.B.

Horse Guards, 25th June, 1855.

SIR,

I am directed by the General Commanding in Chief to transmit to you the enclosed copy of a letter which he has addressed to the President of the Board of Control, drawing his attention to the praiseworthy conduct of Lieutenant Johnson of the 6th Regiment of Bombay Native Infantry, while attached to the 20th Regiment during the operations last year in the Crimea. Lord Hardinge has asked me to furnish you with this letter that you may be aware of Lieutenant Johnson's services, and with the view to recommend him to your notice as an officer fully deserving of any notice you may be enabled to show him.

I have the honour to remain, etc.,

C. YORKE.

Lieutenant-General Sir Henry Somerset, K.C.B.

III.

Lord Hardinge to the President of the Board of Control.

Horse Guards, 25th June, 1855.

SIR,

I have the honour to acquaint you that an application was lately made to me to record Lieutenant

Johnson of the 6th Bombay Native Infantry, for the brevet rank of Major whenever he may obtain his company, on consideration of his having served with the 20th Regiment, from the landing of the army in the Crimea, till after the battle of Inkerman, where he was slightly wounded. I felt it impossible to accede to this application, not only from the inconvenience which has been occasioned by the practise of recording subaltern officers for promotion to brevet rank, as soon as they may become captains, but because it did not appear that Lieutenant Johnson was exercising any other command than that of an officer attached to the 20th Regiment, to none of whom would such an advantage be granted. At the same time papers were laid before me, amongst others a letter from Colonel Horn, commanding the 20th Regiment, addressed to the Chairman of the Court of Directors of the East India Company, speaking in such terms of Lieutenant Johnson as to satisfy me that he had rendered good service while with the 20th Regiment, and particularly at the battle of Inkerman, which was the only occasion on which that Regiment was seriously engaged, and where he was slightly wounded. His zealous desire to see active service, which induced him to proceed to the Crimea, when on leave of absence, merits also high consideration, and I am, therefore, induced to suggest for your consideration whether it may not be proper to make known to the civil and military authorities of the Bombay Presidency, to which I under-stand Lieutenant Johnson is about immediately to return, the claims which by his bravery and intelligence he has acquired to any consideration which the rules of the Service may enable them to extend to him.

I have the honour to remain, etc.,

HARDINGE.

The Right Honourable R. Vernon Smith, M.P.,
President of the Board of Control.

IV.

From Brigadier-General Horn.

16th October, 1858.

I have again much pleasure in certifying to the gallantry of Captain Johnson of the 6th Bombay N.I., who during the Crimean campaign was attached by Lord Raglan to the 20th Regiment, then under my command. It is with much regret that I have just learnt that this very distinguished officer, subsequently engaged in the Persian campaign and Indian Mutiny, has been excluded from the list of recipients of the Turkish Order of the Mejidie, which it appears others of less merit than himself have been decorated with, nor has he obtained any of the foreign orders or distinctive marks which others similarly positioned to himself have obtained. He was present at the battles of the Alma, Balaklava, and Inkerman, and his gallantry was such, particularly at the latter, that I felt myself bound to take special notice of it in a letter to Colonel Oliphant, at the India House, and I now do so again in the hope of obtaining for him the reward of merit, in which unfortunately it appears others have superseded him. If it be not too late,

I shall indeed feel gratified to learn that this deserving officer has obtained one or more of the war distinctions in common with others not more worthy of them. I was on half-pay, and on the staff, consequently unconnected with the 20th Regiment at the time when the list of names went in for such distinction, or Captain Johnson would never have been overlooked by

FREDERICK HORN,
Major-General on the Staff, Malta.

V.

Colonel Evelegh, 20th Regt., to Lieut. W. T. Johnson.

Standen, near Newport, Isle of Wight,
October 7th, 1858.

MY DEAR JOHNSON,

I herewith enclose a certificate of your services, which I trust may be the means of obtaining the Turkish medal for you, which you so well deserve. When, through the late campaign in India, I came across a Bombay man, I frequently asked if you were known, and twice, I think, I heard of you. You and your tulwar I so well recollect. I can see you at this moment going down to the trenches. How the 20th is altered! Poor Butler, I much fear, dying in Dublin; and very shortly I shall be gazetted out, when, I believe, there really will not be one left that you are acquainted with.

Believe me, my dear Johnson,

Yours very truly,

FRED. EVELEGH.

VI.

General Sir Fred. Horn, K.C.B., to Major W. T. Johnson.

1, Redcliffe Road, Fulham Road,
1st June.   No date; probably 1885.

MY DEAR JOHNSON,

Your letter of the 29th reached me this morn-ing, and you could hardly have hit upon a more correct address, for, though living in a neighbouring county (Northamptonshire), Rugby is my post town. Is it not singular that on the very day your letter to me is dated (29th), I called on your cousin, General Turner, leaving one addressed to me from the India House over thirty years ago, on the subject of your gallant behaviour at the battle of Inkerman, and which letter the General will doubtless send on to you. I need scarcely say how glad I was to hear from you, for I have often thought of you, and shall ever remember at that sharp fight, Inkerman, your shouts at the fun, and your swinging your big Indian tulwar over your head, at the charge we made to the barrier,* which gained the old 20th so much credit, when reported to Lord

---

* The charge at the barrier mentioned here was the one described by Kinglake, and quoted in the preceding chapter, when "the air was rent with the old *Minden yell.*" The inlying pickets of the 20th Regiment formed a portion of the first troops sent against the Russians at the battle of Inkerman, and these, together with the remainder of the regiment, were very heavily engaged during the whole of the day. Johnson was with the inlying pickets at the time, and was, as we have seen, twice shot through the clothes, and slightly wounded. It was said to have been "owing to his interposition that the two first guns were brought into action at the battle of Inkerman."

Raglan. . . . I must conclude with my very sincere good wishes, and I am always

Your sincere friend,
FRED. HORN.

VII.

General Sir Frederick Horn, K.C.B., to Mrs. Johnson.

2nd August, 1893.

It affords me great pleasure to reiterate how much I esteemed his extreme gallantry on the field of battle, and during the Crimean campaign, and while he was my aide-de-camp.

CHAPTER V.

AFTER the campaign in the Crimea Johnson received an extension of leave for a few months to see his friends in England, and came home early in 1855. He had a very enthusiastic reception; the bells were rung, and he was heartily welcomed as a Crimean hero. He remained at Enborne for the marriage of his sister, in June, to Mr. Palmer Morewood, and returned to India immediately afterwards. He stayed in Paris, on his way, with his cousin, Lady Louisa Oswald; and from Marseilles went in the *Vectis* to Malta, and on to Alexandria in the *Indus*, making the journey from Alexandria to Suez in vans. He wrote to his mother on board the *Indus*, July 3rd : "We have made up the party for our van, consisting of Chitty and Davis—a couple of fellows in the Indian Navy—a Dr. Oakley, and Fairlie and Adams, of the Bengal Cavalry, and self—rather a jolly party, I think; and if we can lay in a good foundation of iced champagne at Cairo before starting, we shall get on very well. We have a Frenchman who rather amuses us—a perfect tiger to eat; he eats up everything near him, and a great deal besides, and talks about hunting ' wild pork,' instead of wild boars. I have a fellow in my cabin, a little man with a large opinion of himself, going to Calcutta in the sugar and cotton line. He tells me he is going to make his fortune in ten years. I wished him joy, and hoped he would remember me in his will, for old companionship sake. Not that I see how he is to make his fortune, unless he sells himself very often at his own price, and buys himself at mine. We have a band on board, and there was dancing last night. I looked on and smoked a pipe, but thought there was a vast difference between the beauty and fashion on the *Indus*, and at the steeple-chase balls in the Wellington rooms. Every other man seems to be going out to Ceylon to plant coffee."

On July 14th he wrote again to his mother from the *Bengal*, in which he sailed from Suez to Aden: "We were seventeen hours between Alexandria and Cairo, where everything looked as dirty as usual; remained the day at Cairo, and were sixteen hours more in the vans to Suez. In a very few years there will be a rail all the way, which will be more convenient certainly, though I think the trip in the vans, with two mules as wheelers, and the Arab leaders, is great fun. From Aden to Bombay the voyage was made in the *Pottinger*, and she arrived on the 21st July, after a rough passage, being blown along in the monsoon, and losing a boat off Secotra."

On reporting himself on his arrival, he found that he had obtained one or two steps, and was second for his company. He had brought out letters from Lord Clarendon to Lord Elphinstone, and from Lord Beaufort to the Commander-in-Chief, and the letter from Brigadier-General Horn, published to the army in India, was of itself enough to give distinction to any officer. His friends were delighted to see him back without, as he said, "a skewer through his gizzard ;" and he was offered the adjutancy to the cavalry of the Malwar Contingent in the Bengal Presidency. But he was anxious to remain in his own presidency, and as the quartermastership and interpretership of his own regiment were vacant, and he had these to fall back upon, he felt he could wait a while ; moreover, the Adjutant-General had said that no officer could be spared for staff employment, or withdrawn from his corps : so for a time he remained with the 6th at Poona, where he lived with Carr, the adjutant, and his old friend Glasspoole.

In August he received from Colonel Hancock the Crimean medal with three clasps for Alma, Balaklava, and Inkerman, and wrote to his mother: "I am uncommonly proud of it, I can tell you; and it is the first one that has come to this country, so it is thought a great deal more of than it would be in England." Later, in writing to his brother, he said: "I went to dine with the Governor, and found a very swell party —about fifty people—and all the staff. The Governor took tremendous notice of me, and introduced me to the Chief, Sir Henry Somerset; and Lady Somerset got hold of my medal, and handed it about to several of the ladies, and it seemed to be an object of great interest. Afterwards he got me into a corner, and gave me a tremendous pumping about the Crimea, and seemed very much pleased and satisfied. I don't think any subaltern ever received so much attention from the Governor before. Yesterday the Chief asked me to dinner, and was very civil and kind. I suppose, after this, I shall get a good appointment. It seems the Governor has every wish to serve me, and that I had better ask for anything I feel inclined for." In his next letter, from Poona, he says: "I went over to Colonel Hancock, the Adjutant-General, the other day, who told me that my fortune was made, and that I had better wait until I got something good; and he showed me a letter * they had just got from General Yorke from the Horse Guards to the Bombay Government, recommending me to their special consideration : what with this and other letters, I shall be surprised if I don't get something good. The 'Arab's Choice' has arrived in Bombay all safe from Guzerat; but he is not to be raced any more. I see there is some talk of withdrawing more Queen's troops from India and the Cape, and to send out sepoys for garrison duty there. I should not mind going to the Cape—one might get a few elephants and lions there. We expect rather exciting news by the next mail, of some fighting at Kars and Erzeroum and Trebizond. Atwell Lake will be lucky enough to be in for all this, and I shall be very interested to hear all he says. Had I gone there with him, I might have been of use with some Bashi-Bazouks."

In October he went up to Kurrachee to stay with his cousin, Colonel Henry Turner. "If you can fancy," he writes, "a very large cantonment built on a desert of sand, with scarcely a tree or a blade of grass to be seen, you can form a very good idea of Kurrachee; but I don't think it is unhealthy. Henry wanted me to apply for the police appointment here, but I don't seem to care about it; I like to see

* See above, p. 69.

a tree or something green occasionally." On his return to Poona, he found a letter from the Military Secretary, saying that the Governor had proposed him for the appointment of Lieutenant of Police at Aden, for which he would have to pass an examination in colloquial Arabic. He replied that he did not feel his health strong enough, and begged to be excused this appointment. The next day came an official from the Chief with "Immediate" outside, telling him to proceed at once to Jacobabad and take a hundred of the Scinde Horse to Aden.

This despatch must have crossed his letter declining the appointment, for he did not go. He wrote home: "Both the Quartermaster-General and the Adjutant-General, in letters I have received from them, seem to think I was quite right. . . . Have you ever heard of Aden? It is a bare, black rock, and about the hottest place in the world. I was there two days once, and thought to myself, if my regiment was ever ordered there, I would cut my throat. Moore of my regiment has got the appointment, which I am glad of, as he wanted it, and I recommended him for it. He was born in Syria, and is a first-rate Arabic scholar. I feel so delightfully independent, as if they don't give me what I ask for I shall remain where I am, and the appointment of interpreter with the regiment I am holding now, I have to thank no one for, as my passing in two languages entitles me to it. How glad I am to see Atwell Lake getting on so well at Kars! He has made a great name for himself. I wish I had gone out with him ; I should have got another medal then, and one worth having too, but it was impossible to say at that time what would occur. There is no chance of any fighting in India, at least everything is very quiet at present. We have had two or three in-effectual excursions after pig, and I was very much disgusted the other day. We went, a party of fourteen, the largest field I have ever seen, and although we found, we could not get the pig out of the hills, and came home without a run. However, determined not to be done, one of the Rifles and I slipped out the last Brigade holiday and killed two, greatly to the astonishment of the Poonaites, no pig having been killed here for the last two years. I still feel the effects of the Guzerat sun."

In January, 1856, he had a very bad attack of fever at Poona : "I felt exactly as if I had been shot through the head, and the only way I could keep it cool was by holding it over a tub, and having cold water poured over it every hour." At the end of January, the Adjutant-General, Colonel Hancock,

G

offered him the adjutancy and probably the post of second in command of the 1st Battalion Beloochees. He thought it better to accept the appointment, though he did not look forward with pleasure to being quartered at Kurrachee, where there was not a tiger or black buck within hundreds of miles, and very few pig. However, as it turned out, he was not to go there, for a fortnight later he wrote the following letter to his mother :—

"Bombay, February 16th, 1856.

"I can fancy your surprise when you open this, and hear that I am *en route* to Calcutta to join General Outram in Oude. It appears that good luck has come at last, from a quarter I least expected. In a private note from General Outram the other day, he says he has had much pleasure in placing my name before the Governor-General for service with the Oude Contingent, and that he was very glad to find that the Governor-General had had good accounts of me from other sources, and was very glad to serve me, and that I should very shortly be offered the post of second in command of a contingent of Ir-regular Cavalry. The next thing that comes is an official from the Bombay Government ordering me off forthwith to Cawnpore, and on my arrival there to report myself to Major-General Outram, C.B.; so at last, it appears, they have treated me like a gentleman. It is *only* eight hundred and seventy miles from here to Cawnpore—a nice little trip, without roads most of the way. I shall have to do it on horses and camels, unless I go round by Calcutta. I have not made up my mind yet, but I have come down here to buy a couple of good Arabs to take up with me, for one can't get such good ones on the Bengal side as here. Not a bit sorry I did not go to Aden now! I shall get on in Oude, I think, if I have good health, and there is no one I would rather serve under than General Outram."

It will be remembered that he had been on very friendly terms with the Outrams at Sattara in 1847, and at Baroda in 1848. The following paragraph appeared at this time in the papers, in reference to the military organization of the newly annexed kingdom of Oude. " A contingent of some 15,000 men is to be raised: 12,000 infantry, 3000 cavalry, and four companies of artillery, and this will take the place of an army larger than that of England itself, whose services will be dispensed with. The following officers are named as having been appointed: Captain Gowan, Lieutenants Miles and Hawes of

the Bengal Army, and Captain Daly and Lieutenants Black, Johnson, G. Grant, and Hope Johnstone
of the Bombay Army.   By this great concluding act
of his administration, Lord Dalhousie will have
added to the British Empire four provinces of an area
three times as large as the United Kingdom, and a
population scarcely inferior to that of England."

CHAPTER VI.

LIFE IN OUDE. 1856–1857.

LIEUTENANT JOHNSON started from Bombay on the 4th March, 1856, on his long journey to Oude. It was for the most part through native states and a very wild country. He longed to have some shooting on the way, but had to hurry on and report himself to Outram as soon as possible. Oude was favourably spoken of, and tigers and pig were said to be "walking about like cats," so he was in high spirits at the move. The country was in a somewhat unsettled state, but no outbreak was then apprehended. He wrote the following letter to his mother on the march :—

"Bursad, April 4th.

"You will have no idea where Bursad is, till I tell you it is one of the halting-places between Bombay and Lucknow, where I arrived last night, *en route* for

Oude. I have been travelling just a month to-day,
and have as yet only accomplished about two-thirds
of the trip, and find I cannot get on with my kit,
servants, and horses more than about twenty miles a
day. It is a long march : between eight and nine hundred miles, all overland : quite a new country. I feel
going up to Lucknow and joining a new appointment
quite like beginning a new life, and I don't dislike
the idea of it, though it is a nuisance leaving all one's
friends behind in another presidency. This is the
worst of Indian life : one makes acquaintances for a
year or two, and then, just as one begins to find out
the people one likes, one is sent away, perhaps some
five hundred miles.

"Now for an account of my trip, which is rather a
curious one, and so far as comfort is concerned there
is very little. Sometimes I ride, sometimes I put
my bed in a cart, and come along in that way at
night, for it is too hot to travel by day just now ;
sometimes I walk, sometimes come in the mail-cart.
This last conveyance would amuse you, and I assure
you that travelling in one at night is most alarming,
and the excitement even beats tiger-shooting on foot
out and out. The cart is a square red box on two
wheels, with a bar all round to hold on by. Two
horses, one in the shaft, the other attached on the

off-side. The road is bad in places, and very uneven, and it is as much as you can do to see it; but without moon or lamps, away they go, as hard as ever they can lay legs to the ground, change every six miles, and I suppose seldom come to grief. It was the most reckless driving I ever saw; it was as much as I could do to hold myself in with both hands, and the coachman, as he calls himself, keeps on licking the horses from the beginning of the stage to the end, perfectly indiscriminately as to whether they are doing their best or not. There are travellers' bungalows every twenty or thirty miles or so, with chair, table, and bedstead inside, but nothing more. I find the people on the road very hospitable, and wherever there are officers or civilians I am generally taken in and done for, as soon as they find out who I am, and where I am going. I was in a fix on my birthday [March 14]. My servant had made a mistake and had taken all my kit on twenty miles ahead, consequently I had not a single thing; but fortunately a Colonel Browne was marching down with his wife and family, and very kindly asked me over to tiffin, which I made serve for breakfast, dinner, and everything. I see I am posted to the 1st Cavalry; Daly, 1st Fusiliers; and Hope Johnstone, the Commandant and Adjutant, both Bombay officers. Daly is a first-rate officer, a man of great judgment and energy, and we must show the 'Qui hais' how to raise a corps in style. Lord Elphinstone has given me a letter of introduction to Lord Canning, which is more than I could expect, after refusing the appointment he offered me." *

The rest of his march is described in a letter to his brother from Bibiapore, April 29th. "It was a roughish trip of more than nine hundred miles, and in many places, instead of finding travellers' bungalows, I was disappointed and had to put up under a tree, which, as I had no tent, and 150° of hot wind blowing, was anything but comfortable. I was lucky one day in bagging a tigress not far from the road. I got news of a soft place down at the bed of a river ; halted under a tree, and with great difficulty got fifteen niggers out of the villages, who didn't seem to admire the fun much at first. They beat for some time, and

---

* Captain Daly, afterwards General Sir Henry Daly, was one of the most distinguished cavalry officers in India at that time. He raised the 1st Punjaub Regiment at the end of the last campaign, for which he received the thanks of the Directors. He afterwards commanded the Corps of Guides, with which well-known regiment he made his celebrated march from Lahore to the relief of Delhi, in the summer of 1857. He was a very intimate friend of Johnson's, and had the highest opinion of him. "Of all true heroes," he wrote, "none greater than Jehán" (one of Johnson's nicknames) ; and again, "The services of no man, living or dead, better merit recognition than Jehán's."

out came a fine tigress in all her glory. I had
Walker's gun in my hand, but would not take the
chance with that, and had just time to snatch Lord
Craven's rifle from a man a few yards behind and
take a quiet pot at her just as she was passing us,
and bowled her over beautifully. One ball caught
her just below the heart, another just below the
shoulder-blade. She did not seem to like it much,
gave a most uncomfortable roar, but did not come
at us, I am happy to say. She got into some reeds
and bushes, where the niggers particularly wished
me to go after her. We could not find her pugs
anywhere out of the reeds, so surrounded the place,
and found her dead about two hours afterwards.

"I believe had I had time to halt at some other
places I could have had some good sport. I went out
twice : the first day I saw only a sambre ; the next we
found a panther, which went clean away ; we put up
a fine tiger, beating home, which slipped away behind
us. I came through a very wild country, with plenty
of pig ; but both self and horses had enough to do
marching all night, without pig-sticking by day.
One night coming along asleep in a cart, where I had
put my bed, a robber had the impudence to come
sneaking about for anything he could lay hold of,
and caught hold of *my head*, thinking, I suppose, it

was a piece of goods. He pretty soon let go, however, when he found out what it was, and made off, with me after him ; but I could not make much of a run of it with slippers and sleeping-drawers, and I only succeeded in boning the man who was with him, and whom I gave over to the nearest guard-room.

"I got to Lucknow, April 22nd, just the day General Outram left. I missed him by five minutes only; I was sorry not to see him, to thank him for all he has done for me. I found a note from him asking me to go and stay there on my arrival at Lucknow. Lucknow is by far the finest city I have seen in India ; the country is very flat, but is wooded and pretty, scattered over with mango and neem groves; and in some parts not unlike Guzerat. We are only raising the regiment now, and have as yet got only about two hundred and fifty men ; but from what I can see at present, I think it will be a beautiful regiment : the men certainly are the finest I have seen anywhere. We are at Bibiapore, about five miles from Lucknow ; there is one house for all of us ; a good-sized house and six rooms in it—three above and three below. Captain Daly, a Bombay officer of our 1st Fusiliers, is the Commanding Officer, and a first-rate officer he appears to be. From what

I have seen he is the smartest officer I have served under."

He writes again: "My new Commanding Officer and I agree famously, and our ideas on Irregular Cavalry are very similar, and I think in time we shall raise as good a regiment as any in the Service. We have drill parades every morning except Sundays, and anything like the vice of the horses I never saw; they kick and bite anything they come near, and some of them are so bad they are obliged to be kept constantly blindfolded. Our Adjutant, Hope Johnstone, got kicked the other morning; and another horse came a good way out of the ranks on purpose to kick my Arab's Choice, and then went quietly back again. He struck the poor old horse on the fleshy part of the thigh, and did not hurt him much; but he seemed much surprised at being kicked for nothing, and looked round with the white of his eye, as much as to say he would remember him the first opportunity. I wish you could see some of our men: they are so much the most picturesque troops we have; it is the finest branch of the army.

"We are all together in one house by itself in the corner of a wood of mango trees, about five miles from the city. I cannot tell you half enough about Lucknow yet, for the only time (the morning) when it is, cool enough to get out, we are at drill. The heat is something awful, but it is not unhealthy ; and the natives look stouter and stronger and cleaner, and dress better than in any part of India I have been in. We all dine and breakfast together : *i.e.* Daly and his wife, the adjutant, doctor, and myself ; so we are obliged to be very orderly, and put on an extra allowance of manners for the lady. I have a room with the doctor, whose name is Greenhow."

The room they occupied was on the ground floor. The well was a source of amusement to " Jehán," who had inherited a mechanical turn from his father, and used to experiment with a wheel in the watercourse, thinking to get perpetual motion. When he was in Guzerat he had amused himself with inventing and building a cart with very large wheels to go over the sand as lightly as possible ; it was very substantially built to take out in the jungle, with a movable seat, and a pole to put a couple of bullocks in at night: this was at a time when there was hardly such a thing as a made road in Guzerat.

The life at Bibiapore, when raising the regiment, was very quiet. He writes :—

" Generally speaking, the appointment of second in command is the most idle in India, and were it not that we were raising a new regiment, I should have little to do except attend parades. This was one of my reasons for not asking for this line of service on my return to India, for I should much prefer more work and more pay. We get up every morning at 4 for parade; come back about 7 for a cup of tea; breakfast at 10; dinner 7.30; bed 9.30. I have never passed so regular a life anywhere as here, therefore one will have the satisfaction of knowing if one's health fails here, it will not be from want of regularity or temperance. We never have more than one bottle of beer a day (Daly sharing that one with me), half a glass of sherry at two o'clock, and a glass at dinner. Smoking I have given up, except one pipe after dinner. The greater part of the day is spent in reading, making up pattern bridles and saddles, and in carpentering, etc. I have asked to be recommended for the Sattara Police; there is nothing I should like better. Sattara is about the best climate in India. It is in the gift of Lord Elphinstone. At any rate, I shall not stay long in the Bengal Presidency. Our presidency beats it out and out in climate, and I prefer it. I should be sorry to leave Daly and the regiment; and if I were sure of good health, I should not mind remaining."

It was, perhaps, natural to one of Johnson's character that, after a time, his enthusiasm in raising the regiment wore off, and he got tired of the monotonous drill life. Colonel Daly wrote to recommend him for the police appointment, and his having been a good deal at Sattara when the Southern Mahratta Horse was raised, besides having such good testimonials, gave him a very good chance; but events took him elsewhere.

Later, in a letter to his mother, he says: "You will probably read in the papers a great deal of talk of an expedition to Persia, which I fancy will end in smoke. I fancy the state of finances at present won't allow of a war, until there is actual necessity for it. All India seems excessively quiet just now, particularly Oude. The people must be glad their country is out of the hands of such an imbecile old king. I don't know if you have ever read 'the Life of an Eastern King,'* but in it you will read about the palace of the Dilkoosha. It is a pretty-looking building, the centre of a large park, which lies between this and Lucknow; the grounds contain antelope, black buck, blue bulls, monkeys, and peacocks to a great extent—all preserved; and we are at a corner of the park near the banks of the Goomtee; and now

* Knighton (Wm.), "The Private Life of an Eastern King," compiled for a member of the household of Nussir-u-Deen, King of Oude: sm. 8vo, *plates.*

the floods are out, the country is looking perfectly beautiful." This Dilkoosha Palace is interesting, as the place where, a few months afterwards, General Havelock died. It is now only a picturesque ruin.

On the 30th September, 1856, the regiment marched from Bibiapore to Secrora, a distance of sixty-two miles, where they relieved the 5th Irregulars. Just at this time there was a sale of the arms and accoutrements of the ex-king of Oude, and Johnson bought many curiosities in the shape of swords, shields, and matchlocks to decorate his house, all of which were stolen afterwards, together with his favourite Arab's Choice, by the mutineers. He described the march to his mother :—

"*Secrora, October* 21*st.*—We marched from Bibiapore on the 30th, and reached this October 9th ; the roads were bad, and in many places under water and difficult to cross. The Gogra was the worst, and just now, after the rains, it is very much flooded and full of islands and sandbanks. We took three days to cross it, and a very disagreeable job it was. It will give you some idea of what it is like, if you fancy two boats of about forty feet long lashed together, and a platform about twenty feet square on the top of them, perfectly open, without any sort of protection to prevent the horses kicking one another overboard.

If you can imagine this, and then put eight or ten horses on, whose chief object appeared to be to kick and bite one another as much as possible, you will be able to form some idea of what precarious sort of work it was. It is quite marvellous to me that some horses were not smashed. One horse was kicked clean up into the air, and, of course, out into the middle of the river. It did not matter much about their tumbling overboard, for they could always swim ashore on some of the islands, but some tumbled backwards into the bottom of the boats, and were hurt a good deal in this way, but none were killed.

"Secrora is not a very lively place; the society consists of Captain and Mrs. Boileau and his adjutant. They gave us a picnic on the river, and appeared very sociable; and Mrs. Boileau has quite won my affection with the most delicious lobster salad I ever tasted. The chief amusement was fishing, eating, and drinking. Boileau and I were out shooting the other day, and found a few black partridges; they are great beauties, very game birds, something like a grouse, and will quite repay me for the want of society here. There is nothing for any one from Bombay to talk about, except the Persian expedition, and certainly it is very annoying to be out of the presidency now, for, had I been there, I should have had a pretty good chance of being appointed to it in some capacity or other. I sent down two telegraph messages to General Stalker, offering my services with the Irregular Horse, or in any other line more convenient. I can't help thinking that the Shah will give in, and even if the force sails, they may very likely come back again, which would be a bore ; but it would be still more annoying if anything serious were to take place, not to be in it."

Soon after this, Johnson had a serious fall, when out pig-sticking with his friend Doctor Greenhow. He wrote to his brother :—" We had a very successful picnic the other day, and found no end of the bristly, but the ground was awful : long grass full of all sorts of hidden impediments, such as holes, mounds, and blind ditches. The number of purls was quite laughable ; you hear of a man being knocked into the middle of next week ! *I* was knocked into the middle of the last three months, not being able to remember anything that happened during that time. The first thing I remember when I 'came to' was finding myself riding home between the doctor and the adjutant, with a wet handkerchief round my head, and being told that I and the pony had come over in one of these blind ditches, going very fast close to a pig ; and that I had come on my head, and had been talking ridiculous nonsense for three hours. I am thankful it was no worse, and I am all sound again; but I got a terrible shaking. Government has passed me £45 for travelling up here—a wonderful piece of liberality in these days! I am going to invest it in an elephant for tiger-shooting in the Turrai in hot weather; the jungle is so thick that it would be impossible to get on these without one. We can see the tops of the Himalayas early in the morning; I hope we shan't see them in the hot weather, for it would be too tempting—for we can't get there, neither may we go to the tops of the hills: all that country belongs to the Rajah of Nepaul, and they fight uncommon shy of Englishmen since the annexation of Oude. Some of our best politicals never thought favourably of it; but now that it is annexed, there is little chance of the king getting it back again. The Persian expedition, as you will read, has left Bombay. They have given the Shah lots of time to put Bushire in a good state of defence, at any rate."

Johnson was very shortly to join the Persian expedition, and this sketch of his service with the new Irregular Cavalry may end with an extract from a despatch to Brigadier-General Grey, commanding the Oude Force, dated 22nd September, 1856, in which the Chief Commissioner of Lucknow, referring to the

1st Oude Cavalry, expresses his "satisfaction at the state of efficiency which the regiment has attained in so short a period, and the pleasure the Chief Commissioner experiences in being able to submit to Government your commendatory notice of Captain Daly and the officers of the regiment." Captain Daly wrote later: "Major Johnson, of the Bombay Army, served under my command as second in command of the 1st Oude Cavalry, during which time he had charge of the regimental treasure-chest and accounts of the men. A more zealous officer, a more upright, truthful gentleman I never served with. Major Johnson's kindly temper made him a favourite with all, both officers and men."

In November, 1856, war was declared against Persia by the Governor-General of India, Lord Canning, the city of Herat having been taken by Persian troops in defiance of treaties. Preparations were made by Lord Canning, who followed Sir Herbert Edwardes' advice in making a treaty with Dost Mohammad, the Amir of Cabul, and by grants of money and arms helping him to drive the Persians from Herat. The command of the Indian Army was offered to Sir James Outram, who was at the time in England on sick leave; and on his arrival in Bombay, Outram applied for the services of Havelock, to command the Second Division. Havelock was then at Agra, and left for Bombay in January, 1857. Major-General Stalker had already landed at Bushire in December, in command of the land force, and had taken the fort there. Johnson, as we have seen, had telegraphed to General Stalker, offering his services, if he could be spared. In January he received telegraphic orders to join the force in the Persian Gulf, and he immediately went down by mail-cart from Oude to Bombay, and did the journey of 1030 miles in ten days.

CHAPTER VII.

THE PERSIAN CAMPAIGN. JANUARY–JUNE, 1857.

"YOU will be glad to hear," wrote Johnson to his brother, January 7th, 1857, "that I have good chance of employment with the Irregulars under Jacob. A message came from Outram to me yesterday, through Lord Elphinstone, telling me that if the Supreme Government would let me go to Persia, the Bombay Government would place me under Colonel Jacob for Arab levies. Colonel Jacob is one of the best soldiers, and perhaps the most practical man we have, so it will be a good thing for me to serve under him; at least, if they will let me go. You will read all about the fall of Bushire; it seems to have been a much more hollow affair than was anticipated, and it is to be hoped that the Shah received the declaration of war before the bombardment took place, otherwise it may create a sensation at home." The following is the diary of his journey from Lucknow to Bombay :—

" *January* 10*th*, 1857.—Received an order from Lucknow, which had been sent up from Calcutta, to proceed at once to Bombay by dâk* at the public expense, and on arrival to report myself to Government. Sent a small amount of kit off on two shooters (running camels) to Lucknow, to await my arrival; also sent my pony to Nawabgunj, about half-way, to await my arrival. 11*th.*— Left Secrora on the Arab's Choice about 9 a.m., and after taking leave of the Dalys, Greenhow, and Bax (our select little circle), rode down all through the lines to wish our fellows good-bye there, when all the native officers on their horses and ponies accompanied me to Kuttra Ghat. Crossed the river at Kuttra, on to a pony on the other side, and rattled along to the Gogra about eighteen miles; found a dhooly waiting for me on the other side of the river, which brought me into Nawabgunj at 4; on to my pony there, and into Lucknow at 7; and passing Partridge's house found him at dinner. Ate dinner for a quarter of an hour, and cantered on into the city to find my kit, and get a shigram (mail carriage) ready to go on to Cawnpore. Every

* Dâk, *i.e.* post service.

one asleep, and no one inclined to do anything.
Went up to see Lady Outram, and found her with
Mrs. Fayrer at the Residency, just returned from
the hills. Remained there talking till about nine,
and then left in a shigram, very comfortable, and
slept nearly all the way. Arrived at Cawnpore at
9 a.m. on the 12th. Great delay here in getting a
fresh carriage, and did not start until 1.15 ; arrived
next day (13th) at Agra at 8 in the evening ; pitch
dark, rain and thunder-storm ; so thick and stormy
could hardly find the halting-place. Lucknow, 62
miles ; Cawnpore, 53 ; Agra, 179—total 297 miles
in 59 hours : not bad for India. A very hard
beefsteak for dinner at 9.30 p.m. ; wrote three letters,
and sleep.

"Up at 3 a.m. on the 14th, and left Agra at daybreak. No time to see the Taj, or other sights : very
unfortunate, but can't be helped. People say the
Taj is the finest work in India, and that it even
exceeds the anticipation of most travellers. So
much the more my regret, having been disappointed
in most other sights in India. Good road the first
ten or fifteen miles, then sticky mud and heavy sand.
Made road again towards Gwalior—79 miles. Found
that Sir R. Hamilton was there, therefore I knew Bill
Cumming would be with him. Drove up to Cumming's

tent, found they had all gone to a big dinner and Durbar with Scindia. However, Sir R. Hamilton's butler gave me a cold saddle of mutton and a bottle of A1 treble X to wash it down with, and they all returned about ten. Sat up with Cumming, Hunt, and the others till two, and turned in till six. Cumming and I went over and breakfasted with Mrs. Murray, a sister of Mrs. Babington's.

"Left Gwalior at 9 a.m. on the 15th. Sir Robert looking remarkably well, and as hospitable and good natured as ever. Arrived at Ghanaghat at 7 p.m.— 62 miles. Going a sharp canter across country down a very stony hill, one horse came head over heels, or rather heels over head, and got completely under the cart, his head resting against one wheel and his heels against the other. The other horse tumbled over him, and lay resting on some large boulders of rock. A more complete smash I never saw, and how these horses got off without any bones being broken is a miracle to me. After some delay, got them up and harnessed them again the best way we could (one without a bridle, the bit having been smashed in the fall), and came along again as lively as ever. Saw some pretty Brinjaree girls, and, for a wonder, a very pretty cooly girl, who blushed! What next? Very open rocky country, with every facility for road-making ; but this country belongs to Scindia, who does nothing till Sir R. Hamilton makes him. A good road is being made this side of Gwalior, when you go across country again; ground so rough, obliged to hold myself in. Coachman occasionally chucked into your lap. Not pleasant, as they are often greasy and high, indulging plentifully in bad tobacco and garlick. Very unlucky day—only 48 miles.

"Left Ghanaghat at 5 a.m.; arrived at Sipree at 7—24 miles. Breakfasted with Colonel Harris, a very worthy old man and good officer, one whom I would like to see with us up the Gulf; also Wilson, the handsome doctor who lives with him. Left again at 9.30 ; horses all tired and bad ; at a walk nearly the whole way, and English mail tiring all the horses. Only reached Budderwass after sunset ; a stupid, uninteresting country. Colonel Havelock 24 miles ahead of me. This shows the glorious uncertainty of travelling along this road : doing the first 18 miles easy in two hours, the remaining 20 taking me nine. However, I found a large duck, which I immediately turned into the alabaze pan, and made an excellent dinner, and what's the odds, so long as you're happy. Roads very sticky from late rain.

"Left Budderwass at 2 a.m., 17th ; bad roads and

tired horses. Reached Goona at 7; remained half
an hour to grease wheels and have a bit of breakfast.
Came along well to Dewass; good roads, jungly
country. Crossed Parbuttee River; black soil this
side of Dewass; not a bad day altogether. Arrived
at Shahjahanpore at daybreak, 18th; bolted three
eggs and two cups of tea, and came on, doing a very
good day—116 miles. Very pretty tank at Dewass,
but the country from beginning to end is flat and
uninteresting, and becomes warmer and warmer as
you go south. Came from Shahjahanpore to Indore
between 8 and 3. A good road, and horses
better; a good deal of cultivation, but not to be com-
pared in this respect to Oude. Oude and Guzerat
are the most fertile countries I have seen in India;
the former the best.

"At Indore found I could not have a cart, so came
on in a dhooly, starting at 7 p.m. on the 18th.
Came on all night, and arrived at Googra at 8 a.m.
on the 19th; detained here, waiting for kit to come up.
Left Googra at 12 same day; arrived at Shirpoor
at 9 a.m. the 20th; very curious kicking horses all
the way. Left again at 12; arrived at Dhoolia
about five. Went straight to Sam Mansfield, who
gave me some dinner and a bath (how delicious!).
Left again at 9; arrived at Nassick at 3 (21st);

came on straight, remaining a short time at Egat-pooree. Came on at a gallop all down the Thull Ghat, and arrived at Wassing railway station, 50 miles from Bombay. Jumped out of the cart and went to sleep on the grass, pretty well tired out, having rested nowhere for the last 200 miles, except for an hour or two. Found Walker and his wife at the station at Thanna, and Harpur, who came with me to Bombay. Put up at the Adelphi, and went back to Thanna to dine with Harpur."

Notwithstanding this hurried march, Johnson found, on his arrival at Bombay, that he would have to wait there over a fortnight for a transport. He goes on with his journal from the Adelphi Hotel: "Tolerably comfortable, being nicely situated on the race-course, which, as the races were going on, was very convenient. Rather alarmed, after my stay there for a few days, at a married couple and three children—two English girls, one tall and pretty, the other small and plain, also a European servant-maid —all being put in my room to sleep and live there! Rather a curious proceeding, I thought. However, I am used to everything now, and didn't mind it much, except that there was an incessant row, one child squalling incessantly; in fact, I suffered all the inconveniences of a family man for a short time, without any of its advantages. The room was partitioned off by canvas screens into four parts, the two girls occupying the one next to me ; they kept up an incessant talk most of the night, and their ideas were most amusing. A few days afterwards I dined and breakfasted with them at the *table d'hôte*, and got up a desperate flirtation with the pretty one, who I found full of fun and up to anything, when they all disappeared, *viâ* the Cape to England ; and I got an order from the Quartermaster-General to attend at his office for orders regarding some horses to go up under my charge for the Light Field Battery at Hyderabad. So here I am on the *Mirzapore*, one of the Scinde Horse transports, *en route* to the Gulf, *viâ* Kurrachee, where I shall drop these horses and go in this same ship up the Gulf. We are being towed by the *Assaye*, in company with others—the *Alabama* and *Lord George Bentinck*. We left Bombay, February 7th, having shipped the horses without an accident, greatly to my relief.

"*Kurrachee, February 25th.*—I have landed all the horses, I am happy to say, without accident. Captain and crew very civil; they don't care much about h's here. ' 'Ere, 'Arry, those 'orses down in the 'old arn't got no 'ay.' "

The following letter was written to his mother from

Bombay, in addition to the journal : "*February* 22nd. —My last letter will have prepared you for a move in this direction, and here I am in Bombay waiting for a transport to take me up. A day or two after my last letter I received a telegraphic order from Calcutta directing me to proceed at once to Bombay by dâk, and report myself to Government. The literal meaning of travelling by dâk, is being shut up in a box, called in these parts a palky, and carried on men's shoulders. This mode of conveyance doesn't exactly suit my ideas, and as the pith of the order was to get to Bombay as sharp as I could, I came down by mail-cart, and accomplished the trip much quicker than I expected. Receiving the order on the 10th, I started on the morning of the 11th, and reached this on the morning of the 22nd, making it exactly ten days, the distance being upwards of 1030 miles.

"I have had some roughish trips during my life, but nothing ever the least to equal this. Certainly some of these coachmen deserve a medal for the reckless, break-neck way they drive. They go all night, light or dark, moon or no moon, with no lamp. They couldn't go the pace over such ground with lamps. A great part of the way there is nothing more than a beaten track by way of a road : over hills, and through jungles, and across rivers. I shall always look back upon this excursion as the most remarkable one of my life. I was detained in some places by rain, and met with other hindrances I could not foresee, which obliged me to make up for lost time by going all the faster. We came through many interesting places—Agra, Gwalior, Indore,—but of course I had no time to see the lions. They gave poor Colonel Havelock, who was travelling six hours ahead of me, a bad upset into the middle of a corn-field, and bruised his nose and arm a little, but being a small, spare man, he fell light, and is none the worse for it, and has gone on to command a Division. As you may suppose, I had very little sleep all the way, and only one real dinner; this was with a Mr. Mansfield, of the Civil Service, coming through Dhoolia.

"I suppose by this time the Persian War is beginning to create some excitement at home, and perhaps it would have been better had they left China alone, till this Persian business is over. All the best of our men have gone on, as well as the pick of the regiments, and I am looking forward to joining them with much delight, so many of my friends being there. I can't help thinking with many others that the whole expedition is a great mistake, for I can't see any great object to be gained, even should it turn out favourably; and now that the hot weather is coming on, nothing, I fancy, can be attempted on any grand scale, and every one dreads fearful sickness among the troops; but still they go on sending more and more. Somehow or other, people at home, and some out here also, seem to have been seized with a panic all at once that the Russians contemplate an attack upon us; and to prepare for this crisis, we send a force from this country in a totally opposite direction, thereby denuding our frontier of some of our best troops. I suppose it is some grand stroke of diplomacy that we out here know nothing about, and are therefore not able to form an opinion. Mistake or no mistake, I intend to come out with a Brevet Majority, *i.e.* if I come out at all.

"I hear all the thermometers burst at Bushire in June or July. On ahead, towards Bagdad, the climate is better, and I fancy we shall be sent up somewhere in that direction. I should be glad of any maps of Persia, and of those parts of Turkish Arabia neighbouring on the Tigris and Euphrates, and any books or journals you can find that give information on these parts. I have a superb outfit for this campaign, not much in quantity, but very select in quality. I am beginning to think the military profession is not a money-making business, at any rate; all these continual changes make it difficult to keep out of debt.

"Having been obliged to leave all my kit, horses, and servants behind at Secrora, I have to fit myself out afresh. I wish my regiment were going up. The 1st Oude Irregulars would astonish a large amount of Russian cavalry, I think. We despair of any grand affair with the Persians; if they bolt as fast as they did at Bushire, there will be no getting near them. The Persians never could fight yet, and I conclude never will.

"*Journal : March 1st.*—Just at the last moment, as we were under way, got an order to tranship myself from the *Mirzapore* to the *Eliza*, and take charge of all on board. So off I went, and in the dark, my next move after getting safe on deck, was tumbling neck and crop down the hold, very nearly pulling my arms out of their sockets in laying hold of a beam to save myself. After making fast to the *Alabama*, we all three started for Bushire in tow of the *Assaye* steam frigate. We went on quietly enough till Tuesday, when a gale set in dead in our teeth, enough to blow a pipe out of one's mouth, and all that night I felt sure one of our hawsers must snap every minute. However, we rode it out, and anchored off Bushire roads about three p.m. the Monday week following. As far as scenery is concerned, it is by far the most uninteresting coast I have ever sailed along, being nothing but bare rock, without the slightest variety from beginning to end.

" *Tuesday,* 10*th March.*—It blew so hard we were obliged to let out fifty fathoms of chain, and the *Assaye* came drifting by us with two anchors down, but fortunately stopped before she got ashore.

" *Wednesday,* 11*th.*—The more I look at Bushire through the telescope, the more I feel convinced it's the most rotten-looking place I ever saw, and unless it's a very important place for trade, I can't imagine the Honourable John Company sending troops to garrison such a place. If you can fancy a bleak, sandy plain, without a blade of vegetation except a few date trees here and there, that look as if they were ashamed of themselves, and a very dirty town built of mud, and filled with flies, dates, and dust, you will be able to form a very accurate idea of Bushire. Received sailing orders to proceed to Mohamra without delay, under sail. Started at three p.m., and the next morning found us just ten miles from the spot we started from, which shows the glorious uncertainty of the *Eliza* under canvas.

" *Saturday,* 14*th.*—A good strong breeze in our favour all last night ; and this morning ran up the

I

Euphrates and anchored with the rest of the fleet about 4 p.m.

"*Sunday, March* 15*th.*—King and I were sent to report our ships to Colonel Havelock. Went accordingly and met many old friends—McPherson,* of the Highlanders; Hunt of ditto; Nuttall, and several others.

"*Monday,* 16*th.*—The *Agdalia, Golden Era, Suldana, Alabama,* and several others brought up close astern of us. The *Pioneer* came in with news of General Stalker's death. He was a general favourite throughout the whole army; and there could not be a better or more honest servant to Government. In many respects, with his kind and gentle manner, he reminded me of Sir George Cathcart. Heard very bad news: thunderstruck with the intelligence that all the Cavalry and one troop Horse Artillery were to return to Bushire.

"*Tuesday,* 17*th.* — Got under way very much disgusted, and ran down the river; passed the *Mirzapore* aground. Spoke the *Hugh Lindsay* steamer, who told us to 'return,' and received in reply three very loud cheers from the *Eliza.*

"The state of affairs just now is as follows: General Outram is expected every day, when we are to go on and take Mohamra. I send you a rough outline

* Afterwards Sir Herbert McPherson.

of the whereabouts of Mohamra. I dare say it will be a hollow business, after all, but better than Bushire. The *Sybile*, French frigate, which is round here, came down from Bussora the other day, and declared the Persians are full of confidence. However, I look upon their getting a good thrashing as a dead certainty ; nothing can equal the spirits and *esprit* of our corps from beginning to end, and I expect it will be a clasp at least, if not a medal. No one seems to have the slightest idea of the force of the Persians, but probably it may be about 10,000 or 15,000. Our force consists of Her Majesty's 78th Highlanders (7 companies), Her Majesty's 64th (7 companies), one troop Horse Artillery, a Light Field Battery, one squadron Scinde Horse, the Light Battalion of Native Infantry, the 23rd Native Light Infantry, the 26th Native Infantry, and a few others."

The following was to his mother :—" I hope you don't think I ought not to have volunteered for this, because I shall be very much distressed, dearest mother, if I hear that you are in a state of mind about me. Everything must be a trifle, after Inkerman. If I had a wife and brats depending upon my existence, you might consider it decidedly wrong, but as it is, being in the Army, the more work I see of this kind the better. A surgeon, for instance, takes every opportunity of slashing off legs and arms whenever there is an opportunity, and is considered all the more expert in consequence. I sincerely hope this Persian expedition may turn out well, but I certainly cannot look upon it in a more favourable light than the 'Persian folly.' I heard a capital argument to this. A man talking about the Persians and Russians threatening India, said that if a man came to break his door open to rob the house, he certainly would not run out at the other end, and I certainly would not give that old villain Dost Moham-mad twelve lakhs a year to be my door-keeper.

"Regarding the Queen's medal for valour, I shall be very sorry if you try for it: even were there a chance of getting it, I should not take it. I look upon it in this light: If a volunteer or outsider were to serve with my regiment, and get the prize medal, I as a member of the regiment should be very much dis-gusted: and the 20th received me so kindly I should be sorry for anything to occur to damp that feeling."

Johnson was present at the bombardment and taking of Mohamra, which he always described as very tame after the Crimea; and he accompanied the only detachment of Native Horse sent in pursuit of the Persian Army. On the 24th of March the expedition anchored in front of the fortifications of

Mohamra ; on the 26th, fire was opened on the Persian works, the principal magazines were blown up, and the place was taken. On April 5th peace was signed at Paris. The following letter was written on April 19th from the camp :—

"Probably this will be my last from Mohamra, for we all expect shortly to be on the move for Bushire or India. All our prospects of a campaign into Persia are effectually damped by the news of peace, and all I can look forward to now, is a tedious march back to Lucknow. We don't know yet what are the terms of peace, but as far as we can learn, they are not half so good for us as might have been expected, and it is the general opinion that unless it was the intention at the commencement to carry on the war in earnest, it has been nothing more than an enormous expenditure of money and nothing gained. The Persian Army has all gone to ruin, disbanded and broken up ; the state of the country is most thoroughly rotten ; the army, since it has been licked out of Mohamra, has been looted and robbed in all directions, and the Arabs are paying them off for all sorts of tyranny practised on them on their march down. The Government is so thoroughly bad, that I believe many of the tribes would be too glad to be relieved of it, and we could have marched on to Shiraz and Ispahan with very little opposition. Possibly we should have had a fight at the top of the passes, where they would only have run away again, and we should have gone on quite comfortably.

"Last week we got up a little picnic, and ' did ' Bussora, about thirty miles up the river. We hired a native boat and had a very pretty sail, and put up in Mr. Taylor's house, Assistant to the Consul at Bagdad. Most of the place is in ruins, and what with plague and cholera, the place has decreased from about 70,000 to 6000 in the last twenty years, and an intelligent Armenian told me he thought about two more choleras would finish the remainder. The bazaar was better built than the one at Smyrna, and there are some pretty gardens on the river, containing the most delightful conglomeration of fig, vine, date, mulberry, peach, pomegranate, and other trees. Some of the Arabs were such fine-looking fellows ; they came in marketing from a long distance in the desert. They reminded me much of the Circassians you see at Constantinople, only a little darker in complexion. The different costumes and figures you saw in the bazaar made about as picturesque a sight as you could see anywhere—Armenians, Turks, and Kurds with belts full of daggers. The women, as at Cairo and Alexandria, wear a blue veil over the entire face, therefore I can't tell you what they are like ; the people were very civil, and Bussora has not seen so much tin for many a day, as it has since our force has been up here. All the tops of the houses have flat roofs, and in the mornings and evenings this is the coolest place, and we often used to go and smoke our pipes up there. We appeared to attract much curiosity among the Bussora ladies, and we saw numerous heads in all directions, greatly to the indignation of the jealous old Turks. One fellow sent over to say that if we looked at his wife any more, he would cut her throat, or cut his own. We told him to cut his own if he liked, but if he played any tricks with any one else, we should hand him over to the effendi. We heard nothing more of him, but most likely the poor woman got a good licking after we were gone."

The next letter is dated "*Persian Folly Force, Mohamra, May 3rd.*—Here we are still, why or wherefore is more than I can say ; one would have supposed that after peace has been signed, the most sensible thing would have been to send all the troops back to India, before the monsoons set in : but no, they say they must remain here till the treaty is ratified. During my absence here, Daly is transferred as commandant to the corps of Guides in the

Punjaub; and Forbes, of the 1st Bengal Irregular Cavalry, is put in to succeed him in the 1st Oude Cavalry. Had I remained quietly and comfortably in Oude, I should now be commanding the regiment in Daly's absence, and on rejoining the corps I ought to be Daly's *locum tenens*. The news from Mohamra will not take up much room; the most important productions of the place are dates, flies, and fleas: the last to any amount, they come out of the ground in all directions. We have an expedition to Bagdad in contemplation, but I should not wonder if the whole force was out of this by the end of the month. In Bagdad I should expect to see nothing more than Bussora magnified ten times. There is some very fine hog-hunting there, but without horses I don't see how this is to be managed. Lugard, Adjutant-General for Queen's troops in Bombay, is perhaps the best man we have here. There are several good men on the staff. Briggs, Hogg, Cook, and Willoughby having joined our party, we are shortly going to pitch another tent. Several officers have been taken seriously ill after breakfast. You ask what it is, and are told by the authorities it is peculiar to Mohamra to be sick after breakfast. The number of flies affects the food. We have two months of flies, and then two months of an insect of a far worse genus.

Pleasing prospect for us! Thermometer is to be 112° at sunrise, 122° noon, 114° evening."

Just after this they got orders to return to Bombay, and Johnson was one of those told off for the *Dakotah* sailing transport. He wrote from Bombay to his mother, May 27th: "A few lines to tell you of my safe arrival from Mohamra, with several other Bashi-Bazouks. Nicholson, an old Guzerat friend of mine, going down sick ; Nicholetts, Leith, Neave, and Bradford, made up the rest of our party, with 162 horses and a quantity of bullocks. All of these, being senior officer on board, I had to look after, and the heat sometimes was something so awful it was fortunate the horses arrived safe. We came down part of the way in tow of the *Semiramis* war steamer, and then, after putting in at Muscat to coal, it began to blow so hard that we were obliged to let go and sail. We found Muscat a better place than we expected : it is situated something like Balaklava, land-locked in the same way, only the cliffs not so precipitous. We landed and 'did' the place satisfactorily. We found the town about as dirty as Bussora, full of Arabs and Persians. At Muscat we found some bad fruit, which to us was a great treat; where it came from we could in no way comprehend. When we asked, they pointed in the direction of a mass of rocks without a blade of cultivation of any kind : you see nothing but range over range of bare rocks all round you.   I am thinking of starting for Calcutta June 1st. Not having seen any papers since the 14th of April, you will learn more from them of the rows in the North-West than I can tell you."

CHAPTER VIII

THERE had been for some time rumours of disaffection among the sepoys in the North-West Provinces, and news of the outbreak of mutiny among the native regiments at Meerut, Ferozepore, and Delhi, had by this time reached Bombay. General Havelock had arrived at Bombay from Persia, and was anxious at once to hurry overland to join the Commander-in-Chief, who was believed to be marching on Delhi ; but the risks of doing so were great, and Lord Elphinstone would not permit it ; so Havelock had, instead, to go to Galle in the hope of catching there the mail steamer for Calcutta. He left Bombay on the 1st of June, in the P. & O. steamer *Erin*, with Captain Baily; his son (young Henry Havelock), Johnson, and a few others with him. Johnson wrote to his brother from the *Erin*, off Cochin, June 4th—"You will wonder where in the world I have got to now, so I'll tell you. I am on my way to Galle to catch the big steamer from Cochin to Calcutta, and am going on from thence to the North-West Provinces to shoot Bengal sepoys. I remained in Bombay a week, and intended to have taken a run up to Poona to see the regiment, but on account of this row all our services are required with our respective regiments in Bengal, and I thought it best not to delay. So here we are, on board the *Erin*, the ship that ran down the *Pasha* some years back off Singapore. We left Bombay on the 1st, and expect to be at Galle to-morrow, where we shall move into the *Bengal*, which will take us up to Calcutta in eight or nine days or so. The *Erin* is tolerably comfortable: commissariat very good, except the tea, which is a go between that article and coffee. However, as much good claret as you can drink supplies the deficiency without grumbling. Such curious critters by way of servants—Chinese without eyes, and with most glorious pigtails, down to the bottom of the calf of the leg; they are very clean, and make excellent servants. Our party consists of General Wilson, Havelock (Adjutant-General for Queen's troops in Bengal), young Have-lock (his son), and a few others, merchants of sorts for Ceylon and Shanghai. Not a bad party altogether, and having beautiful weather, we have as yet had rather a jolly trip than otherwise.

"I suppose this disgraceful mutiny has created great excitement in England as well as in India. The worst of it is, I hope, over now, although the accounts were but seedy when we were in Bombay. Nothing to create any alarm has occurred, I am happy to say, on our side of India, and I dare say if a little grape had been scientifically administered in the first instance at Meerut, it would have put a stop to all further proceedings. When it is all over, I dare say it will do good in many respects. It will show the Bengalese that their system of soldiering is quite a mistake, at any rate, and create an entire reform, which was much wanted. I am not the least afraid of any of the Irregular Cavalry turning against us; in fact, the mutiny has been solely brought about by the Bengal Infantry of the line, and the sooner these fellows are hanged the better. It is just what you might expect in an army where the officers are afraid to keep up a sufficiently strict discipline amongst their men. Have you seen the very mild orders that have come out from the Governor-General? It is not much to the purpose to *ask* mutineers to keep quiet. The only way it will be done, is to show them you can make them give in. Rather an unfortunate occurrence took place just before my departure from Bombay. I had just drawn about seventy pounds from the Pay Office to pay my way back to Oude, brought it back, and put it into my writing-case, and a negro coolly walked off with the whole of it! Rather inconvenient, just at starting, and there is not the slightest chance of ever recovering a farthing of the money. How curious India will be after this mutiny! Of course no more ladies will come out; you have no idea what attention will be paid to the army now."

In the envelope of this letter is written: "We have just been shipwrecked, but all hands on shore safe." The *Erin* was wrecked on the west coast of Ceylon, a few miles below Colombo, off a small village called Kalutara South. The coast is very dangerous, with many reefs and sandbanks; it was a very bad time of year (June 7th), and she struck at night. The captain was in his cabin, and it is said that the officer was misled by his compass, which was a new one; but as it went to the bottom nothing could be proved. A star had been taken, and the course was supposed to be right. Fortunately the sandbank on which the *Erin* struck was near the shore. It may still be seen, just opposite to the little village of Kalutara, and quite recently one of the paddle-wheels of the unfortunate vessel was visible in the sand. It was through Johnson's presence of mind, which never failed him in time of need, that the alarm was given. He was the first to hear the breakers, and to assist in sending up blue lights and rockets, and in firing off the gun. He lost most of his kit, which was in the hold, and there was not time to get it out before the ship went to pieces. The Commander, Captain Baily, is still living at Colombo as agent to the P. & O. Company there (he is well known as the best judge of precious stones in the island). In writing about " Billy " Johnson's conduct at the time, he says : " I remember him well : we were both comparatively young men when the *Erin* was lost, and his behaviour at the time fixed him in my memory. I thought he was the pluckiest man I ever saw. He was below when the saloon was half full of water ; got his powder-flask out of his revolver case, and stood with the sea rushing over him, and primed the gun which we were firing. We had got cartridges up, but the priming powder was wet." Johnson's own letter to his mother gives a graphic account of the shipwreck :—

> "On board *Fire Queen,*
> " 125 miles S.E. of Madras..

" Rather an unfortunate termination to my trip

with the 'Persian Folly,' to be first robbed of seven hundred rupees, and immediately after to be shipwrecked, instead of more honours, and a Brevet Majority, as I expected. I won't grumble though, for 'misfortunes will occur in the best-regulated families,' and perhaps we are very well out of it, for had we struck a mile north of Kalutara, it would have been the last you would ever have heard of the old *Erin*, 'Master William,' and all the rest of us. Joking apart, I assure you we are all very thankful it was no worse; for to end one's career by being drowned like so many insignificant kittens, it is not exactly what one would prefer, to say the least of it. And now you will like to know the particulars, which I will condense as much as possible. Well, you already know we were *en route* between Bombay and Point de Galle on board the *Erin*, iron paddle P. & O. boat, running between Bombay and China. On Friday afternoon, took the sun as usual, and found ourselves a hundred and sixty miles from Galle ; took the sun again at four the same afternoon, and a star at ten, and then the captain turned in. We were running then under topsails, with the current in our favour, eleven and a half or twelve knots an hour.

"Young Havelock and I were sleeping in our usual

places on the top of the skylight. The least thing
awakes me sleeping, and about one, hearing a peculiar
noise, I sat up and listened, and thought to myself
we must be in shallow water, amongst a lot of
breakers. Havelock saw me sitting up, and asked
me what was the matter; but I did not answer him,
not knowing what *was* the matter. Just then a heavy
shower of rain came on. I rolled up my bed like a
shot, and sung out to Havelock if he did not look
sharp he would be washed down in five minutes. I
had been below only three minutes, and had turned
in again under the stern window, thinking that I must
have mistaken the noise of the rain on the water for
breakers, when, first, came a very slight bump, then
two together—bump, bump; then bang, bump, a roll
and a dash simultaneously; and so we went on being
dashed about till the end of the chapter, expecting
the ship (iron) to go to pieces every minute, and not
knowing in the least where we were, which made it
much worse; and not being accustomed to being
shipwrecked, I thought the position most particularly
disagreeable, and felt a very peculiar sensation,
commonly called 'funk,'—very much what I felt at
Inkerman when I found myself alone, surrounded by
Russian riflemen, all deliberately shooting at me.
Every one looked particularly astonished; there was

K

a great deal of rushing about, much jaw, but very little done. Blue lights and rockets were sent up *ad libitum*, but no reply from the shore. At last, knowing the habits of niggers ashore in a storm, how they roll themselves up like hedgehogs, seeing nothing, and hearing very little, I suggested that we might fire off one of the guns on board ; and I assisted to get up some blank cartridge (which we did with difficulty) ; but these not being rammed home sufficiently, made but a poor report ; however, it was the first they heard of us ashore. It was not of much consequence, however, for nothing could be done, or rather nothing *was* done, until daylight. What amused me most was, during the commotion, a man in a great state of excitement, ramming his head into my stomach, with a ' Here you are, sir,' and putting a bundle of shotted cartridges into my hand, by way of some blank ammunition for the gun ! Fortunately I felt the shot inside, or we should the next moment have astonished the village with a volley of grape.

"Well, in the morning boats put off and took us ashore, and most of our baggage ; and they got the specie out and the mails, and about nine the poor old *Erin* broke in two, with about £150,000 of opium on board, and most of the ship's officers' baggage. After she began to break up, the scene on shore was highly ridiculous—every sort of thing being flung overboard in the hope of its being washed ashore—chairs, boxes, beds, cushions, a cow and calf, sheep, cocks and hens, ducks and geese (these seem to vote it rather a lark than otherwise), a horse (who didn't). Poor Baily, the captain, was very much cut up about it: he had only been in command about six months. The officer on watch was to blame, for not keeping his eyes and ears open when the squall came on. . . . I think, had the wheel been put over immediately the ship struck, she might have been saved; but they stopped and backed engines, which was useless, as we were going under topsails twelve knots an hour. The rudder was smashed very shortly after we struck. So much for this. If you look on the map, you will find a place on the west coast of Ceylon, about half way between Colombo and Galle, called Kalutara. We found very comfortable quarters; Mr. Templar, the judge, took us in and did for us; and the same night we went on into Galle. We were too late, how-ever, for the steamer, which had gone on to Calcutta the day before; so we got a lift up in the *Fire Queen*, which had been sent down from Calcutta to Galle for European troops; but there being no Europeans to send from there, she was ordered back, and to touch at Madras. I lost some of my silver kit and camp kit on board the *Erin*, which will put me to some inconvenience. It was down in the hold, and they could not get it out. Such a dirty steamer this, and cockroaches as big as young rabbits."

On his arrival in India he found that he had suffered still greater losses, for, in his absence, all his household goods—horses (including his beloved "Arab's Choice"), and everything he possessed—had fallen into the hands of the mutineers. Amongst his treasures was a very valuable collection of armour and weapons; and for all these losses he only received compensation in part.

He arrived at Calcutta in the *Fire Queen* on the 17th June. Sir Henry Havelock, and Sir Patrick Grant, who was then Commander-in-Chief at Madras, were on board. Sir Patrick presented Havelock to Lord Canning with the words, "My Lord, I have brought you the man;" and Havelock was forthwith despatched to support Sir Hugh Wheeler and Sir Henry Lawrence, who were holding the mutineers at bay at Cawnpore and Lucknow. The dauntless and heroic Neill had already gone on with his "Lambs"—the 1st Madras Fusiliers—and had quelled the outbreak at Allahabad.

On June 25th, Havelock left Calcutta, he and his little band travelling by rail and road to Benares.

Johnson, on arriving with Havelock at Calcutta, had received orders from Lord Canning to proceed up country, and officiate as second in command of the 12th Regiment Irregular Cavalry. He accordingly went up to Benares, but was unfortunately attacked there with severe illness. He had been very ill while he was at Calcutta, and in the doctor's hands ; but he made light of it, and hurried on as soon as possible. He wrote to his mother from Benares, July 14 :—

"You will be surprised to see my letter dated from Benares, but I came up here a few days since, intending to drop down the river to a place called Chupra, and from thence to Segowlee (where the 12th Irregular Cavalry were) ; but, unfortunately, I am laid up here with my side troubling me again, and having had leeches and a blister on yesterday, I am quite unable to move out of bed. The pain, however, is nothing serious, and I shall be well, I hope, in a few days ; but it is a bore just now to be laid up, during the present state of affairs, when every Englishman is wanted for work. . . . Matters in this part of India just now are looking up, and General Havelock has given the mutineers a good thrashing between Allahabad and Cawnpore, and will march on and relieve Lucknow. I should have gone on with him, had I been well. Several men from Oude are here just now. Boileau from Secrora is one ; you have heard me speak of him before ; he is the husband of the lady who used to make such lovely lobster salad. He has lost everything, except his wife and children (who are safe in Lucknow), and the horse he rode away upon. All my things were plundered at a place called Nawabgunj, between Secrora and Lucknow, so I have not the slightest chance of ever seeing them again—four rifles and a gun, swords, shields, and many trophies of much value. The 'Arab's Choice' and the brown Arab colt are supposed to be safe in Lucknow.*

" As to my regiment, it has gone ; a few Sikhs only remain. In fact, the whole of the Oude Contingent has mutinied, almost to a man—three regiments of cavalry, ten of infantry, three batteries of native artillery, and about two thousand police. Doesn't it sound ridiculous ? and Sir Henry Lawrence holding his own at Lucknow all this time with a few Europeans. I regret very much being absent when the thing occurred. I think I could have held some of the men together, at any rate ; but there is no saying ; perhaps I might have been decapitated like the rest. I should have been commanding that party that started under Hayes (Military Secretary

* They were never recovered.

to Sir H. Lawrence), who was murdered with Barber, Fayrer, and the others. The slaughter amongst officers, women, and children has been awful ; and I don't expect the country will be quiet till we have had remuneration by blowing away from guns some twenty thousand. It is a sad thing ; and I can't help thinking that many an innocent victim will suffer, who has been misled by these cowardly lying villains. However, there is only one way to treat a mutiny, otherwise there is an end to all discipline for the future.

" Holmes's * troops have mutinied as well as the Gwalior Contingent. The former from Indore marched on Mhow, and old Platt, with the 23rd, a battery of artillery, and some of the 1st Cavalry, gave them a most awful licking. The most curious state of affairs exists now in India—the greater part of the Bengal Native Army have all gone mad at the same time. Government calls it a Mussulman row, but I believe myself that the most bigoted of the Brahmin Hindoos are the mischief-makers, and that the Mussulmans do the fighting part of the business. They are a much more open race than the Bengal Brahmins. One article will be much

* He was Commandant of the 12th Irregular Cavalry, of whom Johnson later took command.

required in India when the troops arrive : *i.e.* small powerful river steamers, drawing but little water ; with a good supply of these, the work could be done in half the time, not only for troops, but for heavy ammunition, commissariat stores, etc."

Johnson lay at Benares sick for several weeks, and during this time the state of affairs had become much worse. Havelock reached Allahabad on the 30th of June, where he met Neill, who was there equipping the advance column, which left the same afternoon, under the command of Major Renaud, for Cawnpore. Havelock intended to follow with a stronger force on July 4th, but was delayed three days by the task of forming the Corps of Volunteer Cavalry, which afterwards did such fine service under Barrow. On July 7th Havelock marched from Allahabad with the main column, and marched (as an old sergeant of the 84th Regiment told the writer) "fighting all the way." But before their start, sad news had come of the massacre and destruction of the gallant little garrison of Cawnpore. Havelock's "Ironsides" did not number two thousand men. But what they lacked in quantity was made up in quality, for finer soldiers never stepped. Their first battle was at Futtehpore, July 12th—Havelock's first engagement as a General in command. Eleven guns were taken. The next was at Cawnpore, fought on the 16th of July, and on the following morning the English took possession of the station. But, alas! they were just too late.

It will be remembered that after the massacre at the Ghat (of which tidings had been received by Havelock on the 1st of July) the unfortunate women and children had been taken back to Cawnpore, and confined in a single bungalow by Nana Sahib. When he heard of the approach of Havelock's column, he ordered them to be immediately slaughtered. First, the men, of whom there were but few prisoners, were brought out and killed ; and then he sent down the sepoys of his guard to shoot the women and children. It is said that they fired over the heads of the hapless prisoners ; at all events, few were killed ; so the Nana sent for some butchers out of the city to finish off the work with knives. The ghastly tale is told by Mr. Shepherd, a civilian resident in Cawnpore, in his narrative of the siege. He writes :— *

"The native spies were first put to the sword, and after them the gentlemen : they were brought out from the out-buildings in which they had been confined, and shot with

* Mr. Shepherd's narrative was shown to the writer by Professor G. W. Forrest on her voyage home from India in 1895, and the extracts were made by his kind permission.

bullets. Then the poor females were ordered to come out, but neither threats nor persuasions could induce them to do so. They laid hold of each other, and clung so close that it was impossible to separate them, or drag them out of the building. The troopers, therefore, brought muskets, and after firing a great many shots from the doors and windows, rushed in with swords and bayonets. Some of the helpless creatures in their agony fell down at the feet of their murderers, clasped their legs, and begged them in the most pitiful manner to spare their lives, but to no purpose. The fearful deed was done deliberately and completely, in the midst of the most dreadful shrieks and cries of the victims. There were between a hundred and forty and a hundred and fifty souls, including children. The doors of the building were then locked for the night (16th July). Next morning it was found that some ten or fifteen women had managed to escape by falling or hiding under the murdered bodies of their fellow-prisoners. Fresh orders were therefore sent to murder these also ; but the survivors, not being able to bear the idea of being cut down, rushed out into the compound, and seeing a well there, threw themselves into it without hesitation. The dead bodies of those murdered by the butchers on the preceding evening were then ordered to be thrown into the same well."

Another account of the scene is given by a sergeant of the 57th, who went with Havelock and Neill into the house of blood, a few hours after the massacre. He relates that the Nana, when he heard of Havelock's pushing forward, ordered all the prisoners to be killed, and appointed a hundred of his men to kill the men, and a hundred more to kill the women and children, and served out a hundred rounds of ammunition. These men fired upon the poor creatures, but, it is supposed, missed them intentionally by firing over their heads. So the Nana sent into the city for some thirty of the lowest caste men—butchers—to kill them with knives. They were men of a low outcast tribe, but even of these degraded creatures only five would do the frightful work. Three of the five were faint from heat and blood, and only two remained to finish it. One of them fell into the hands of Havelock's soldiers, and he confessed that he had broken three weapons in the ghastly work, and finished off with a cavalry sword. He said he was forced to go on by the Nana's men.

All this took place at the very time that the battle of Cawnpore was being fought outside. When Havelock's men entered the city they were righteously maddened by what they found. The floor of the house where the women and children had been confined since the massacre of the men at the Ghat, rather more than a fortnight before, was a pool of blood. All round the walls were the marks of the bullets and the stains of blood, with tresses of hair, articles of clothing, letters, toys, ornaments, and other piteous relics. The soldiers followed the tracks of blood which they found on the grass outside, and traced them to the brink of the well, which had been covered by the sepoys with branches of trees, in the vain hope of hiding it from the English. They found it full to the brim with the mangled and mutilated bodies of English women and children—some dead, some dying—all thrown in together. Is it a wonder that the vengeance taken was a terrible one—that the soldiers were driven almost to desperation?

Neill's retribution was merciless. He forced the highest caste men to lick up the blood, which, according to their creed, would send them to destruction: then many of them were blown from guns, and the tree stands now, on which numbers were hanged. Even Havelock said, "Are there not some prisoners? do they not encumber us?" It took his men several days to bury the dead: some in the well, some in another well, which had been the scene of many a gallant deed, some in another large grave, and some in a small cemetery close by what was the House of Blood. Often there were three and four in one grave. The House of Blood was razed to the ground: it was not thought right that it should be left standing. Over the well, and hiding it from view, stands now the Memorial—a lovely angel of spotless white marble,—and around the base runs this inscription: "Sacred to the perpetual memory of a great company of women and children who near this place were cruelly massacred by the followers of the rebel named Dundhoo Puath, but commonly called Nana Sahib of Bithoor, and cast, the dead with the dying, into the well below, A.D. July 16th, 1857, and in graves close by." On one cross is the appropriate inscription: "Our bones are scattered at the grave's mouth, as when one cutteth and cleaveth wood upon the earth." The ground all round the Memorial is consecrated, and close by is the Memorial Church, dedicated to All Souls, the walls of which are entirely covered with marble tablets to the memory of the victims of the massacres. Beside the Memorial, stands the tree where hundreds of mutineers were hanged by Neill's orders. In the peace and beauty of the scene it is hard for the visitor to Cawnpore of to-day, to realize the piteous tragedy of the spot.

CHAPTER IX.

THE MUTINY—AFFAIR AT HUTGAON WITH THE BOATS, UNDER MAJOR VINCENT EYRE, SEPT. 10, 1857.

LIEUTENANT JOHNSON, as we have seen, was lying ill at Benares during the time that the terrible things related in the last chapter happened. On the 5th August he wrote the following letter to his mother from Benares: " Altogether things in general have a much worse appearance than when I last wrote : in fact, the whole of Bengal is in the most delicious state of rebellion you ever heard of, and it strikes me the whole matter must end in a big campaign in the cold weather, or rather as soon as a sufficient force comes out from England. I hope to be at the fall of Delhi yet. Up to the last accounts Delhi was not likely to fall for some time. Some of our best men have been wounded there. Neville Chamberlain has been dangerously wounded. Daly also, I am sorry to say, has been wounded, with many others.

The last accounts, too, from General Havelock are not good : he had been obliged to halt for reinforcements, and the mutineers have broken down a bridge before him. Havelock has about 2000 men with him. The enemy have probably 10,000. They make every sort of difficulty to prevent his advance, and Havelock will have to fight his way by inches. However, I expect to see him come out with flying colours. He is a very fine old fellow, settles down in a fight, and becomes as cool as a cucumber.

" People here look as if they would like to eat you raw, bones and all. However, the whole country now had better have its mutiny, and then there will be a reaction, decidedly a considerable reaction, when 10,000 troops from England begin to make an advance in the cold weather. Just now all Europeans work under a sad disadvantage, on account of the heat ; besides, the country is half under water, and it is impossible for an army to move except on the Grand Trunk Roads. There is only one good road between Cawnpore and Lucknow ; if Havelock gets off this he finds himself immediately stuck in the mud. The loyal 12th Irregular Cavalry have gone : they distinguished themselves by killing the Commanding Officer Holmes, his wife and family, and the doctor, his wife, and family ; and had I not been detained here by weakness, there is not the slightest doubt what my fate would have been. You know I was on my way to join Holmes. I have heard from private sources that I have been appointed commandant of a new yeomanry corps of cavalry to be raised, and am daily expected in Calcutta. I have received nothing direct from Government, but shall write about it to-day, for perhaps they do not know where I am. I am better than when I last wrote, but not able to move yet."

The following despatch refers to this appointment :

"Council Chamber, Fort William, Calcutta,

"August 4th, 1857.

"SIR,

"I am directed to request that you will have the goodness to order Lieutenant W. T. Johnson, of the 6th Bombay Native Infantry, lately doing work with the 12th Irregular Cavalry, and who is believed to be detained in or near Benares, to proceed immediately to Calcutta, for the purpose of being appointed to the command of the Bengal Yeomanry Corps.

"I am, etc.,

"R. I. H. BIRCH, Colonel,

"Sec. to the Government of India,

"Military Department.

"To the Officer commanding, Military Department, Benares."

Johnson was at this time ordered by his doctor to go home for change, and his cousin, Colonel Henry Turner, wrote about him as follows : " I have written strongly urging him to go home, and I do hope he will follow my advice ; we must be thankful that his illness prevents his being in the midst of these horrid mutineers, where his life would be often endangered when least expected. His regiment of cavalry is one of those that has mutinied, and three of the officers with it (and their families) were murdered. Thank God Billy was not with them ! He is quite safe where he is, and in Bengal we may hope that the worst is over. We shall ere long hear that Lucknow has been relieved, and that General Havelock's force has gone on to reinforce the army in front of Delhi."

The following letter was written by Johnson to his mother on August 18th, from " The Mint, Benares." " Not a letter have I received from England for nearly three months, so I suppose these have all been looted by these beggarly mutineers. The mail from England is just in here, *via* Calcutta. At last I am glad to see the mutiny is beginning to create some excitement at home, and I have just been reading the speeches after the first arrival of the news in England of the Meerut affair, and the siege of

L

Delhi. Disraeli in some respects seems to take a pretty correct view of the case; the Earl of Hardwicke more particularly so, in recommending troops to be sent overland at once. Had troops been sent overland in the first instance, they might now be on their way up the Indus, having disembarked at Kurrachee. They would by this means get water transport as far as Mooltan. Reinforcements for the Force now before Delhi would reach us much sooner in this way than *viâ* the Cape and Calcutta; I should say six weeks sooner.

"And now for the mutiny out here. I don't think matters are much worse since I wrote last; sixty-two regiments of Native Infantry, eight of Regular Cavalry, seven of Irregular Cavalry, the whole of the Oude, Gwalior, and Indore Contingents having mutinied, and being all loose about the country, you can fancy there is rather a confusion in the state of affairs in general; and the whole of the country from the Punjaub down to the Hoogly is in a most unsettled state at present, and will remain so for some time to come, I am afraid. It is difficult to give people in England, who have never been in India, a correct idea of what is going on, but perhaps you may gain some little insight from the following remarks. Although almost the whole of the Bengal

Army has mutinied, I don't think mutiny is at all the feeling of the country at large, and I feel there is hardly a village throughout the disturbed districts that would not be too glad of a settlement of affairs, to be as they were before. Just now they are all living in a most uncomfortable state of alarm, being liable to be plundered and insulted in every way, by bands of these brutal mutineers and rebels, at present wandering about the country.

"To show you that the peasantry are not against us: when all the Oude mutineers went out to fight General Havelock on his march to Lucknow, the villages from without came in and supplied the garrison of Lucknow most handsomely with provisions. Also at Delhi, our camp is supplied with all the necessaries of life, when the mutineers are in great want within the city. The men who have mutinied have made themselves enemies on all sides ; the country people and villagers they have robbed and otherwise ill-treated, hate them ; all the old pensioners ditto, because, if they gain the day (which there is no chance of), what will become of the pensions ? Now the beggars have mutinied they don't know what to do. They can't work together, and they get licked whenever they come across a force under European discipline.

They can loot small villages, and destroy property and life where there is no opposition, but nothing more. Most of them have gone to Delhi, and I have heard lately that the Mohammedans and Hindoos have been fighting amongst themselves there, which I think very probably is the case.

"Regarding the settlement of matters again in Bengal, it is a question of tin, guns, and ammunition. As long as we can keep treasure, big guns, and ammunition from falling into the hands of mutineers, we shall have the advantage; but with the country in this state we should, I think, find great difficulty in collecting revenue in the disturbed districts, and I am afraid for a short time this will prove a great drain on England. When once established, and a better system laid down with respect to the expenditure of the revenue, I hope the country will thrive more than ever; there will be no more sepoys to pension, no King of Delhi, and no petty Rajahs to eat and swindle away the revenues. I shall wind up now, or you will declare I speak like a book, or am writing a sermon on the subject; but since these two great nations—England and India—have become so dependent on each other, it is impossible not to think seriously on the subject.

"General Havelock found himself so hard pressed

on his advance into Lucknow, he has turned back and recrossed the Ganges into Cawnpore, where he remains for reinforcements : in the mean time reinforcements on the river are detained at Dinapore to go up the Gogra under Outram. The country up to the end of September between Fyzabad and Lucknow is impassable for artillery, on account of swamps and rain. At any rate, a movement in this direction must delay the relief of Agra. If Agra is allowed to fall into the hands of the mutineers just now, it will most materially delay the settlement of that part of the country round Delhi. There are no end of ladies at Agra ; two or three siege trains, besides kits of ammunition, and I dare say a good lot of treasure. If they concentrated the troops at once at Cawnpore, and then went on at once to Agra, and from there reinforced our army before Delhi, it might shorten matters considerably. Lucknow could hold out, until another force came to the relief *vià* Cawnpore.

"This is most fearful weather for the poor European soldiers to work in : it is the climate they have to fight, not the mutineers. I am much better ; side nearly well. A telegram came to me the other day from Lord Dunkellin, Military Secretary to the Governor-General, to say that if Lieutenant Johnson

was anywhere near Benares, he was required immediately in Calcutta, to take command of the Bengal
Yeomanry Cavalry. I sent back word that I was too
sick just then, but I trusted I should be fit for duty
very shortly. This is very flattering to me, and the
pay would probably be £100 a month. Unfortunate
my being sick just now; when they hear I cannot take
it at once, they will very likely put in some one else."

This was his last letter from Benares. Shortly afterwards, Sir James Outram, who had been appointed
to the military command of the Dinapore and
Cawnpore Division, passed through Benares with reinforcements for Lucknow. Johnson was, as we have
seen, ill at the time, and his doctor had ordered him
to go home; but he was not the man to shirk duty
or danger. He knew that General Outram had no
cavalry of any sort when he arrived at Benares, and
was also aware how greatly General Havelock was
feeling the deficiency of cavalry at Cawnpore. He
therefore requested permission of General Outram to
accompany his reinforcements, and proposed to make
the attempt to bring up, by forced marches, all the
men of his regiment—the 12th Irregular Cavalry
—who remained faithful. The greater part had
mutinied, as we have seen, but a remnant were faithful
under Russeldar Muhammad Bukah Khan. General

Outram at once accepted Johnson's offer of his services, and gave him instructions to bring up this remnant and all of the regiment that he could muster without delay, and join him by forced marches.

Johnson started the same day, and proceeded to Azamgarh, with an escort of only two horsemen: brought the remainder of the regiment up, and by forced marches joined the column even sooner than he expected. This was when the rebellion was at its height: nearly the whole of the Irregular Cavalry in Bengal had mutinied: the officers in his own regiment had been killed, and when he joined the force he did it at the risk of his life. General Have-lock said openly, "Johnson is a great fool to trust himself with these men ; they will be sure to cut his head off some day." But the young officer had great influence over natives. He trusted them, and they believed in him. This remnant of the regiment stuck to him stanchly throughout, and he commanded them in all the engagements between Cawnpore and Lucknow, under Generals Havelock and Outram.

Subsequently, at the Alumbagh, the remnants of the 12th and of the 3rd Irregular Cavalry served together. They performed many valuable services, and so much did their behaviour meet with the approval of Govern-ment, that after the relief of Lucknow, every one of

Johnson's men received a step of rank in promotion, besides a reward in money of a hundred rupees ; and the senior native officer under him received a special mark of appreciation, in the shape of a sword of honour, from the Governor-General.

The following letter, from General Sir James Outram, written somewhat later, shows his opinion of the regiment :

"MY DEAR JOHNSON,

"Colonel Napier has shown me your note, and I answer it myself. I most highly appreciate the conduct of the detachment of the 12th Irregulars : first, for the faithful devotion they have displayed to the Government when all others of their class, and even of their regiment, were faithless ; secondly, for their gallantry since they have come under my command ; and you may depend upon my doing ample justice when, in my reports to Government and the Commander-in-Chief, I have the power to promote, and to confer the order of merit, and shall be most happy to promote every man to such rank as you may please to recommend, as well as to confer the order on such as you may consider to deserve the distinction, on your furnishing me with a nominal roll ; and this I would do in the most public manner on a general parade, as I also purpose doing to the native troops of the garrison. I doubt whether you have the power to promote, as you purpose; but if you have, and would prefer doing it yourself to my doing so, you may.

" Sincerely yours,

" J. OUTRAM."

Outram wrote again, December 28th, 1860: " Major Johnson, of the Bombay Army, commanded a corps of Irregular Cavalry in the force under my command during the operations connected with the relief of Lucknow Residency and re-conquest of Oude, 1857–8, and I most willingly record my testimony as to his great worth as a gallant and zealous cavalry officer. Besides showing the utmost activity and forwardness in the field on all occasions, he lost no opportunity (and he had many) of rendering me efficient aid in miscellaneous services, which demanded the exercise of intelligence and zeal. Thus, during the time we were shut up in the Residency, he was most useful in obtaining information, and accomplishing important objects, by means of the Sikhs under his command."

The men's rewards were well deserved, for they were the few out of many thousands that remained faithful to Government. The 12th Irregular Cavalry were the only native cavalry at the relief of Lucknow. In speaking of this forced march, Johnson used to say, "It was the most difficult duty I ever performed during my military career, but it was also the most successful."

The following letter to his mother describes this period :

"Camp Gopeegunj,
"Halfway between Benares and Allahabad,
"September 6th.

"I am writing regardless of the departure of mails and everything else; but I am so delighted at receiving a packet of sweet letters from Enborne, I feel obliged to write a line out of sheer joy, not having received any for more than three months. I think it is a hard case I am to be scolded so much for losing my money. You all seem to take it to heart much more than I did. I intend to take the change out of these natives before long.

"I wrote last from Benares; since then General Outram passed up through there with reinforcements for General Havelock, and ordered me to bring up all the remaining portion of the 12th Irregular Cavalry, and to join him with all speed, either at Allahabad or Cawnpore. So off I started the same day; dropped down the Ganges to Ghazeepoor; rode up to Azamgarh; arrived there late on the evening of the 1st September. Took command of the regiment (or rather of all that is left of it), and issued an order to be ready to start at two the next morning. This Bombay way of doing business seemed rather to astound the Bengalese. They made all sorts of excuses not to start; but we *did* march, and precisely at two; and here we are at Gopeegunj, and have done twenty miles a day ever since. Diarrhœa has been bothering me again. I have had it more or less ever since I left; but I am better now, and hope I shall not knock up. I want to see us well through this mutiny, and then come home for a long time, for I am sure my health requires it. I would not like to leave India just now; in fact, if I possibly can, I intend to be at the relief of Lucknow, and the more rebels I am able to kill, the more happy I shall be. I never experienced such a wish for revenge for the deaths of so many of our countrymen as I do now. I dare say it is very wrong, but I can't help it.

"I shall send this off at once, for I have lots of work on hand, as you may suppose. We march at eleven or twelve at night, and don't get to our ground till seven or eight in the morning. The weather is much improving. I think you will hear of

an effectual smash in the mutiny ere a fortnight after
you receive this. We came up from Ghazeepoor to
Azamgarh with an escort of only two sowars.* Met
with nothing but civility from the country people ;
they were awfully civil, alarmingly polite. They
were quite the contrary a month ago. My sowars,
however, are all very 'koosh,' † and have behaved
famously as yet. However, I am perfectly liable to
have my throat cut at any moment, but I don't
anticipate it. I received such a kind letter from
Holmes ‡ just before his death. I must send you a
copy of it some day ; I have time for nothing now
except duty."

About this time he received the following note
from Sir James Outram :

"Camp Kurranea [no date], 1.30 p.m.

"My dear Johnson,

"Though your note is dated 7.30 a.m.,
those rascally horsemen have only this moment
brought it in, and so have forfeited the hundred
rupees reward I promised them. Captain Dawson,
who takes this note to you, will explain the object of
your *dawr*, and will accompany you to Hutwa Pass,
the place of rendezvous with Major Eyre, who has

---

* Horsemen.   † Happy.   ‡ C. O. of the 12th Irregulars.

with him twenty guns and a hundred and fifty
Europeans. We calculate that Hutwa Pass is about
ten miles from your camp; thus your men will have
done forty miles in one day, which I shall long remember in their favour. But I am disappointed to
find you have only forty men. Where are all the
others? If their horses are done up, their best plan
will be to follow our march leisurely, and overtake us
as convenient. We shall be to-morrow at Futtehpore.
You will of course remain with Eyre, who will overtake us before we reach Cawnpore, or, at any rate,
before we cross the river. I send you my own watch,
set to our time.

" Sincerely yours,

"J. OUTRAM."

On the 10th September, Captain Johnson, in command of the 12th Irregular Cavalry, and Lieutenant
Charles Havelock, second in command, joined Major
Eyre at Hutgaon. Major Eyre had been sent on by
General Outram to make a *dawr*, and attack a party
of insurgents from Oude, who had crossed the Ganges
near the village of Koondun Puttee. As they were
approaching the rebels, he sent Johnson on to
account for them, who hastened with all speed to the
spot, and found the enemy had reached their boats

with a view to escape across the river into Oude. Johnson was only just in time to dismount his men, and use them as riflemen. Had he been five or ten minutes later, the rebels would all of them have escaped. He had not even time to link the horses together (though they were so done up with the heat and forced marches, that there was but little risk of their straying), but opened fire on the mutineers at once, which they returned; and he succeeded in holding them in check until Eyre came up with two companies of Her Majesty's 5th Fusiliers, when short work was made of them, and but few escaped.

This successful expedition was the means of preventing a daring invasion of the territory through which the Grand Trunk Road passed, which, at that critical time, it was of the greatest importance to keep open. Here was one of those occasions in which Captain Johnson's ready wit and presence of mind stood him in good stead. Had he not, on the spur of the moment, turned his cavalry into infantry and held the rebels at bay, they must all have escaped. It was a position where cavalry could not act, and when Johnson arrived the mutineers were in the act of pushing off their boats. It was, moreover, a position of great risk, for the odds were as 300 to 40. Had the mutineers charged, the little force must have been annihilated, the enemy would have got away, and the communication with the base of operations would have been cut off.

APPENDIX TO CHAPTER IX.

THE FOLLOWING DESPATCHES FROM GENERAL, OUTRAM AND MAJOR EYRE RELATE TO THE ACTION AT HUTGAON.

I.

Major-General Sir James Outram to the Deputy Adjutant-General.

Camp, Thureedon, 11th September, 1857.

I have the honour to report, for the information of His Excellency the Commander-in-Chief, that on arriving at my camp, Katogun, on the 9th inst., I received definite information that a party of insurgents from Oude, amounting to from three to four hundred, with four guns, had crossed the Ganges near the village of Koondun Puttee, fifteen miles north of Khaga, on the Trunk Road between Futtehpore and Allahabad. On joining Major Simmons' column at this place, I despatched, under Major Eyre, a party consisting of a hundred men of H.M.'s Fusiliers, fifty of H.M.'s 64th, mounted on elephants, with two guns, and completely equipped with tents, two days' cooked provisions, and supplies for three more. Captain Johnson's detachment of the 12th Irregular Cavalry, consisting of forty men, made a forced march, and concentrated with Eyre's party at Hutgaon Khas yesterday evening, having completed forty miles. For the further proceedings, I beg to refer His Excellency to Major Eyre's despatch. His reputation as a successful leader had been already so well established, that I purposely selected him for this duty, in the perfect confidence that he would succeed. The importance of his success will, I am sure, be fully appreciated by your Excellency and the Governor-General. I now consider my communications secure, which otherwise must have been entirely cut off during our operations in Oude, and a general insurrection, I am assured, would have followed throughout the Doab, had the enemy not been destroyed, they being but the advance guard of more formidable invaders; from which evils having been preserved by Major Eyre's energy and decision, that officer and the detachment under his command are, I consider, entitled to thankful acknowledgment from Government, which I am confident will not be withheld.

II.

Major Vincent Eyre, commanding a Field Force, to Colonel Napier (afterwards Lord Napier of Magdala), Military Secretary.

Koondun Puttee, September 11th, 1857.

I am happy to have it in my power to report, for the information of Major-General Sir James Outram, that the expedition he did me the honour of entrusting to my command has been attended with entire success, and the daring invasion of this territory from Oude has been signally punished. I arrived at Hutgaon last evening at dusk, where I was joined by Captain Johnson's troop of 12th Irregular Horse, forty in number. As they had marched twenty-four miles, and were in need of rest, I halted till half-past one a.m., when we had the advantage of moonlight to pursue our march to Koondun Puttee, where we arrived at daybreak. The Oude rebels, having been apprised a little previously of our advance, had fled precipitately to their boats, about half a mile off. I ordered the cavalry under Captain Johnson and Lieutenant Havelock to pursue them, and followed myself with all practicable speed with the infantry and guns. We found the cavalry had driven the enemy into their boats, which were fastened to the shore, and were maintaining a brisk fire on them from the bank above. On the arrival of Hill's Fusiliers and 64th Foot, under Captains Johnson and Turner, the fire of our musketry into the densely crowded boats was most telling; but the enemy still defended themselves to the utmost, until the guns under Lieutenant Gordon opened fire, when the rebels instantly threw themselves panic-stricken into the river. Grape was now showered upon them, and a terrific fusillade from the infantry and cavalry was maintained, until only a few scattered survivors escaped. Their number appeared to be about three hundred. Previously to their plunging into the river, they threw their guns overboard, and blew up one of their boats, where, I regret to say, one man of Hill's (54th) was killed, and ten more or less injured, of whom five were Europeans and five natives. All the officers mentioned above distinguished themselves highly, and the conduct of the men was all that could be desired. Lieutenant

M

Impey, of the Engineers, and Mr. Volunteer Tarbey have likewise by their zeal and usefulness merited my thanks and commendation.

P.S.—Having heard of another party of rebels at the Ghat, higher up the river, I have despatched the cavalry to reconnoitre.

III.

Extract from Major Vincent Eyre's Despatch on the following day.

September 12th.

In the postscript of my despatch of the 11th inst., I mentioned having sent the forty of the Irregular Cavalry troopers under Captain Johnson to reconnoitre, and if possible to intercept a party of Oude rebels, said to have landed at Ukree Ghaut.

They had, however, retreated across the river, before Captain Johnson's troop could get at them, but a small fort that had been recently erected by the rebels was destroyed by Captain Johnson. I was informed by Mahomed Zuboor Khan, the Thanadar of Koondun Puttee, that, had not the Oude invaders been checked, and a portion of them destroyed by our troops, it was their intention to overrun the whole country between Futtehpore and Allahabad, with a view of interrupting our communications and impeding our operations. . . . I take this opportunity of mentioning that the detachment of the 12th Irregulars had already marched twenty-four miles when they received the sudden order to join me at Hutgaon ; and although the men and horses had been a whole day without food, they galloped on the whole way to meet me, a distance of nine

miles farther, guided by that energetic officer Lieutenant
Dawson, who also took a conspicuous part in their
subsequent operations.*

IV.

General Vincent Eyre to Major Johnson.

Hotel des Bains, Boulogne-sur-Mer,
27th March, 1871.

Your letter of the 23rd reached me on Saturday, and
recalled old times, when I had the privilege of being enabled
to render some service to the State, through the agency of
good soldiers like yourself, who both knew what was to be
done and how to do it.

On the particular occasion in question, I perfectly well
remember how much I was indebted for the success at-
tendant on your promptitude in driving the Oude rebels
to their boats, and there holding them in check until the
arrival of the infantry and guns to complete their destruction. In my despatch given at the time, I endeavoured to
render full justice to yourself and young Havelock.

V.

The action with the boats is thus referred to in Marshman's " Life of Havelock," p. 394 : " At Hutgaon Major Eyre
was joined by Lieutenant Johnson, the commandant, and
Lieutenant Charles Havelock, second in command of the

* Extract from General Orders from the *Government Gazette :* " The
conduct of Major Eyre and his officers was highly appreciated by His
Excellency the Commander-in-Chief and the Governor-General in
Council."

remnant of the 12th Irregular Cavalry, forty in number, who had remained faithful to Government. They had hastened from Benares by forced marches to overtake Sir James Outram, and when they joined Major Eyre, had been twenty-four hours in the saddle, and required rest. The major halted his little force until an hour after midnight, when it recommenced its march, and came up at daylight with the enemy, who immediately fled to their boats and endeavoured to recross the river.

"Lieutenant Johnson, with prompt decision and great judgment, dismounted the greater portion of his men, and by a continued carbine fire, succeeded in preventing the removal of the boats till the European infantry could come up.

"In announcing this action to the Commander-in-Chief, Sir James stated that a general insurrection would have followed in the Doab, or province lying between the Ganges and Jumna, had not the enemy been destroyed, they being but the advance guard of more formidable invaders."

VI.

Extract from Recommendation Rolls.

Lieutenant Johnson, 6th Bombay Native Infantry, commanding 12th Irregular Cavalry, highly distinguished himself in Major Eyre's attack on the rebels at Hutgaon, and in the advance to Lucknow.

(Signed) D. S. DODGSON,
Deputy Assistant Adjutant-General.

Umballa, 20th July, 1858.

VII.

The Secretary to the Government of India, Military Department, to the Deputy Assistant Adjutant-General.

With reference to your letter of the 16th inst., forwarding Major Eyre's account of his successful operation against a party of rebels who crossed from the Oude side of the Ganges into the Doab, I am directed to acquaint you, for the information of His Excellency the Commander-in-Chief, that the Right Honourable the Governor-General in Council highly appreciates this further good service rendered by Major Eyre and the detachment under his command, and has noted with satisfaction the energy and sound judgment exhibited by Major Eyre and his officers in the execution of it.

CHAPTER X.

BATTLE OF THE ALUMBAGH AND SIEGE OF LUCKNOW.　SEPTEMBER 15-25, 1857.

IT was dusk on the evening of September 15th when General Outram arrived at Cawnpore. Two days earlier Captain Johnson, with his loyal troopers, chiefly Sikhs and Punjaubees, all splendid fellows, had joined the column, as also had Lieutenant De la Fosse * and his three companions, the sole survivors of the siege of Cawnpore, who had escaped after the massacre at the Ghat. They swam six miles down the Ganges, until a friendly Rajah allowed them to go ashore, and gave them shelter. When he gave them leave to go away, they just happèned to fall in with the relieving force.†

---

* Now Major-General De la Fosse, C.B.

† Lieutenant De la Fosse had, during the siege of Cawnpore, earned the sobriquet of "De la Fosse of the burning gun," in the following manner, referred to in the narrative of Mr. Shepherd, a civilian of Cawnpore, and quoted in Mr. G. Forrest's "History of the Mutiny."

Generals Outram and Havelock met at Cawnpore, only three months after their parting on the abrupt close of the Persian Campaign, and Outram, with a chivalry and generosity which have seldom been equalled, waived his rank, gave up the command to General Havelock, and accompanied the force to Lucknow in his civil capacity, as Chief Commissioner of Oude, tendering his military services to General Havelock as a volunteer only, and joining the Volunteer Cavalry.

We have seen how Havelock arrived in Cawnpore on the 16th July. He had been waiting there for reinforcements up to now. On the 16th August he

---

"This day," Mr. Shepherd says, "I saw a very daring and brave act done in our camp about midday. One of our ammunition waggons in the north-west corner was blown up by the enemy's shot, and whilst it was blazing, the batteries from the artillery barracks and the tank directed all their guns towards it. Our soldiers being much exhausted with the morning's work, and almost every artilleryman being either killed or wounded, it was a difficult matter to put out the fire, which endangered the other waggons near it. However, in the midst of all the cannonading, a young officer of the 53rd Native Infantry, Lieutenant De la Fosse, with unusual courage, went up, and lying himself down under the burning gun, pulled away from it what loose splinters he could get hold of, all the while throwing earth upon the flames. He was soon joined by soldiers, who brought with them a couple of buckets of water, which were very dexterously thrown by the lieutenant, while the buckets were taken to be replenished from the drinking water of the men close by. The process of pitching earth was carried on amidst fearful cannonading of about six guns, all firing upon the burning waggon. At last the fire was put out, and the officers and men escaped unhurt."

had marched to Bithoor, where an obstinate battle took place ; the enemy lost two hundred and fifty killed and wounded, and the English loss was forty ; but Havelock's men were so exhausted by sunstroke and cholera, that on their return to Cawnpore many fell out on the road to die. His force, indeed, had been fearfully reduced ; sickness, constant fighting, and cholera, had made terrible ravages amongst them, and they were much too weak to attempt a march on Lucknow until reinforcements came, which was not until a month later.

About this time Johnson wrote the following letter to his mother :

" With the Oude Field Force,
" September 18th, 1857.

"I write you a line, perfectly regardless of mail departures, but probably shall not have much time to myself for the next six or seven days, when I hope to be able to tell you we have relieved Lucknow. We are now going to cross the river ; six guns, some Sikhs, and two companies of Highlanders are already across. But it is no joke crossing a river like this with such an army. A bridge was made across the river in three days, a bit of engineering that has never been done before in the face of an enemy. If it were only a month or two later, the weather would be beautiful ; as it is now, it is awful for Europeans ; but every one is in excellent spirits. I don't think the work between this and Lucknow will be as severe as some people suppose, and I hope the 12th Irregulars will distinguish themselves. I've got the command, and they are the only native cavalry in the field ; therefore, as you may suppose, I have a delicate game to play. They behaved very well the other day with the affair at the boats on the Ganges. Had we not been there the infantry would have seen nothing of them till they were well out of shot" (for particulars see Major Eyre's and General Outram's despatches of the 12th and 13th September*). " I think some of the 13th Irregular Cavalry have been given every encouragement not to serve the Euro-peans ; but General Outram is much in my favour, and supports me. I am quite sure that it is of the greatest importance, that the native soldiers who have remained faithful, should now meet with every encouragement on the part of Government. The enemy over the river get only four pice a day ; they are very short of large ammunition. They have several guns in position ; we shall take them. Their bullocks, horses, and means of carrying away their guns are bad. I could write you such a long,

* Given in chap. ix., Appendix.

amusing letter, with so much interesting news. My health is better. I hope to last till the relief of Lucknow. With the blessing of Providence, I hope we may get through this duty without any severe loss."

The army under the command of General Havelock (Outram having waived his rank) numbered 3179 men, all told. It was composed of the 84th Regiment, with two companies of the 64th attached, the 5th Fusiliers, and the 1st Madras Fusiliers, under the command of General Neill ; the 78th Regiment, the 90th Light Infantry, and Bradyer's Sikhs, commanded by Colonel Hamilton. The Artillery Brigade consisted of Maude's Battery, Olphert's Battery, and Eyre's Battery of 18-pounders, under the command of Major Cooper. Barrow commanded the Volunteer Cavalry, and Johnson the Native Cavalry. Captain Crommelin was Chief Engineer.

The column began its march from Cawnpore on September 20th, and at once successfully engaged the enemy at the village of Mungulwar, and on the following day (the 21st) at Busseerutgunj. On the 22nd they halted at Bunnee, on the Sye, and Havelock ordered a royal salute to be fired, hoping that the sound of it would reach the ears of those anxiously waiting in the Residency at Lucknow, but the wind was not in the right direction. On the 23rd they marched on again to the palace of the Alumbagh—a park and pleasure-ground of one of the princes of Oude, about five miles from Lucknow; and here it was that the battle of the Alumbagh was fought.*

"The enemy's line extended nearly two miles, and was supposed to consist of 10,000 men, while a body of cavalry, estimated at 1500, was massed on their right. The General was anxious to turn their right flank, but they had planted themselves, as they had often done, behind a morass, and the turning movement could only be accomplished by a considerable circuit. To cover this operation, the General brought up his heavy battery of 24-pounders and his two 8-inch howitzers.

"The enemy's guns, which were masked by trees, had preserved silence during the reconnaissance; but as the advancing column came within their range, a withering fire was opened, from which our troops suffered to some extent. But the heavy battery came up, and, deploying on a dry spot on the left of the road, soon succeeded in silencing the enemy's artillery, and in driving back their cavalry. They stood the shock of this heavy ordnance—so rarely seen in the field—only for a few moments, and then broke up in confusion. Our troops and guns followed them as closely as the nature of the ground would permit. But one of their

* Marshman's "Life of Havelock," p. 403.

guns, planted on the road, and admirably served by the well-trained artillerymen of the Oude Force, still continued to send destruction among our troops, when Lieutenant Johnson, by an act of gallantry not surpassed in any action during this campaign, without waiting for orders, charged it with twenty troopers of his Irregular Cavalry, sabred the gunners, and silenced the gun. Finding himself unsupported a thousand yards in advance of the Force, and the enemy keeping up a galling fire from neighbouring cover, he was compelled to abandon it and retire; but the dread inspired by this dashing charge deterred the enemy from serving it again, and the troops were free from its molestation during their further advance."

Johnson's gallant action in taking this gun is thus described in Mr. Archibald Forbes's "Havelock," p. 184: "Outflanked on their right and their centre and left, crushed by the fire of Eyre's heavy guns, the rebel army began to break. But there obstinately remained in action on the road one of their guns, which was admirably served by the well-trained gunners of the Oude force, and whose fire had bowled over several of Johnson's Irregular horsemen. Johnson was an extremely practical young man. With a dozen of his troopers at his back, he galloped up the road a good thousand yards out to the front, rode straight on to the obnoxious gun, sabred the gunners, pitched the ammunition into the ditch, and the gun after the ammunition, and then cantered quietly back, till he met the main body on its advance. In all this campaign there was no pluckier action."

Just after the battle of the Alumbagh, the news was received by General Outram that Delhi had fallen. He immediately announced it to the troops, and, as an eye-witness of the scene told the writer, "such a cheer was raised as might almost have been heard in England."

The following letter, from Johnson to his mother, mentions the affair with the gun at Alumbagh, in which he took so active a part: "General Havelock has mentioned my name, for nothing except volunteering and making myself generally useful. . . . Outside, at the fight at Alumbagh, my men really had some fun, and behaved uncommonly well. When we left Cawnpore I had only about fifty men and native officers; and just before the action of the Alumbagh, on the 23rd, I was ordered to send half my detachment back to look after the baggage, which was threatened with cavalry; thus I was obliged to send poor Warren, my adjutant, back with half the men, greatly to my disgust and his too. No one seemed to care a straw about the baggage when we all expected a general action on ahead. Well, on we went—galloped through a bit of water with the Volunteer

Cavalry, and took one gun, without the loss of a man, I believe, and then stood still to be shot at. I was under Barrow, who was my brigadier. We were not long before starting again; and I knew the next best thing to do was to take the next gun, which had been bowling 9-pounders at us for the last half-hour or so, down the road. So at it I went with my five and twenty men. Greatly to my relief, they never fired a shot as we came on; and we took the gun without much difficulty. We chopped up a few of the men, and the rest ran away. . . . I only lost one man killed, and a few men and horses wounded: my own mare got a shot through the hock."

As we come to the account of the first relief of Lucknow, it may be well briefly to refer to the events which had taken place there up to this date. At the time of the annexation of Oude, in February, 1856, Lucknow was one of the finest cities in India. It was densely populated, and filled with temples, mosques, and palaces of the greatest magnificence and beauty, and had a large number of wealthy inhabitants. Owing to the hopelessly bad government of the whole province, the king was deposed and pensioned by the British Government, and finally went to Calcutta, in March, 1856. For a time things went smoothly, but early in May the following year a mutiny broke out amongst the native troops in Lucknow, and a little while later the mutiny at Meerut took place.

Sir Henry Lawrence, the Chief Commissioner of Oude, had recently been appointed Resident at Lucknow, and he did all he could to prepare for the storm which he saw was coming, by collecting supplies and stores, fortifying the Residency and Muchee Bhawun, and bringing in the ladies and children, and the boys of the Martinière College, into the Residency. These boys were in time trained into soldiers, and afterwards proved of the greatest use during the siege.

On the 30th May, 1857, the native regiments in Lucknow all broke out into open rebellion, and the troops at the out-stations followed. But it was not until a month later, on the 30th June, that the actual siege began. On that day the ill-fated battle of Chinhut took place, at a village about eight miles off, whence (it had been reported to Sir Henry Lawrence) a small body of rebels were about to march on Lucknow. He determined to meet them, and marched out at 6 a.m. with this object. But the European force was vastly outnumbered ; the heat was intense; the native artillery drivers deserted to the enemy ; the native cavalry took to flight ; and the result was disastrous. Our troops had to retreat, fighting all the way, and closely pursued by the enemy; the workmen employed on the Residency fortifications deserted, the supplies were stopped, and the Residency was placed in a state of siege, in which it remained four and a half months.

On the 2nd July Sir Henry Lawrence was wounded by a shell, which burst in his room. On the previous day a shell had fallen in the very same spot, and Sir Henry was urged to leave the room and go to another; but he laughingly refused, saying "he did not believe the enemy had an artilleryman good enough to put another shell into that small room." He was removed to Dr. Fayrer's house, and lingered in great agony until the 4th of July, when he died. He was buried in the churchyard close by, " with the men," as he desired; indeed, at that time many were buried in one grave. On his tomb are the simple words he himself wished to have there: "Here lies Henry Lawrence, who tried to do his duty. May the Lord have mercy upon his soul."

The incessant cannonading went on day after day, and week after week, and constant and desperate attacks were made on the Residency. On the 20th July a mine was exploded near the Redan, and the mutineers boldly advanced, but were repulsed with much loss. On the 10th August, on the 18th

August, and on the 5th September, assaults were
made and repulsed ; and every day and every night
the ceaseless fire of cannon and musketry went on.
Brigadier Inglis, who had succeeded Lawrence in
the command, wrote as follows of this time :

"The whole of the officers and men were on duty during
the eighty-seven days that the siege lasted, up to the 1st
relief. In addition to incessant military duty, the force was
nightly employed in repairing defences, moving guns, bury-
ing the dead, and in fatigue duties too numerous to mention.
Notwithstanding all their hardships, the garrison made no
less than five sorties, in which they spiked some of the
enemy's heaviest guns, and blew up two of the houses from
which they had kept up their most harassing fire. Each
man was taught to feel that on his own individual efforts
alone depended in no small measure the safety of the whole
position. This consciousness incited every officer, soldier,
and man to defend the position assigned to him with such
desperate tenacity, and to fight for the lives which Providence had entrusted to his care, with such dauntless
determination that the enemy, despite their constant attacks,
their heavy mines, their overwhelming numbers, could never
succeed in gaining one single inch of ground within the
bounds of the straggling position, which was so feebly
fortified, that had they once obtained a footing in any
of the outposts, the whole place must inevitably have
fallen."

The patience and courage shown by the women

N

were marvellous, all through those anxious days. No place was safe; all were alike exposed. Cannon balls and bullets passed through doors and windows; houses were constantly blown up, and even the rooms of the banqueting hall (turned during the siege into the general hospital) were completely exposed. The sick, wounded, and dying were, however, throughout devotedly nursed by the ladies.

One of the mutineers, an African rifleman, nick-named "Bob the Nailer," was stationed on a turret of Johannes's House, just outside the walls. This position commanded the road, and extended as far as the general hospital, and Bob's aim was so unfail-ing, that literally no one escaped him. It was im-possible even to cross the road, except when he was loading his rifle, and it was equally impossible to hit him, because he was protected by the turret. At last it was determined to blow up the house by a mine, which was carried under it from the Martinière Post, and Bob the Nailer perished in the explosion.

The horses and other animals suffered terribly from hunger during the siege, eating each other's tails off, as in the Crimea. The following anecdote was told to the writer by a woman who was in Lucknow all the time. She sent out her native servant one day to let loose a gentleman's horse, which was tied up. The man did not return, so they went to look for him, and he was found lying dead. The starved horse had seized the poor fellow by the back of his neck, and had bitten his head off. In August the entire garrison was put on reduced rations; the women had three-quarter rations, the men and children half; this allowance was later on still further reduced, and the necessaries of life were at a fabulous price.*

The present writer, when recently visiting Cawnpore and Lucknow, found it almost impossible to realize the fearful scenes of the past. The Baillie Guard Gate, Aitkin's post, Dr. Fayrer's house where Lawrence died, the Residency itself, with the cellars underneath, where the women and children were kept, the Treasury and the post-office, both scenes of the sharpest conflict—all these historic ruins are still standing. The crowded churchyard where Lawrence and the other heroes lie, is close to the Residency, though the church itself was entirely destroyed during the siege. It must be remembered that the Residency grounds were simply surrounded by a mere wall, and the houses of the city came up so close to the line of defence, that the Sepoys within the

* Some prices are given in Johnson's letter below, p. 192.

entrenchments could talk to those without, and the rebels were constantly heard mocking the loyal troops. Night alarms were very frequent, and it was at night that the men had to repair defences and bury the dead. Their numbers, too, became so reduced that each man felt that an enormous responsibility rested on him, and each man, therefore, behaved like a hero. There were several places at which a dozen men abreast could have entered—so feebly was the position fortified—and this would no doubt have happened but for the dread the mutineers had of the extraordinary pluck and courage of the "Sahibs."

On the 16th August, Sir John Inglis wrote a very urgent letter to General Havelock, describing the straits they were put to, and imploring help. Havelock replied, "I can only say, hold on and do not negotiate, but rather perish sword in hand." Weeks went on, and no news came from the outer world. The death rate for many days averaged twenty, and still the brave little band went on, hoping against hope, for the help that seemed so long to tarry.

CHAPTER XI.

HELP came at last. On the 23rd of September
the sound of artillery was heard in the direction of
Cawnpore, and the next day the heavy guns of the
relieving force were recognized. The force started
from the Alumbagh at eight a.m. on the 25th of
September, after a day's rest. There was a choice
of roads; the first was by the Charbagh bridge,
and thence on in a direct line for about two miles
to the Residency. This was the shortest route, but
it was so strongly defended that it could only be
taken as a last resort. The second was round by
the Dilkoosha Palace, and along the bank of the
Goomtee river. The third was a middle course
between the two; by this they would first force
the Charbagh bridge, then turn to the right, and
go along the bank of the canal to the bridge on the

road to Dilkoosha, and then turn sharp round to the left, towards the Residency.

The last was the route taken. At the Charbagh bridge there was heavy fighting, and young Havelock was wounded, but the bridge was won. The next desperate struggle took place at the Motée Mahal. The heavy guns were brought into service, and the column suffered heavily. From the king's palace, the Kaiserbagh, the battery manned by Oude gunners was doing terrific damage; but the High-landers dashed in, killed the gunners, and spiked some of the guns. It was here that Outram and Havelock had a difference of opinion about the advance. Outram proposed to halt, to enable the rear-guard to come up. Havelock, on the other hand, wished to push on without delay. "Let us go on, then, in God's name," said Outram; and go on they did, but it was at a heavy cost; of the entire force—some two thousand—about a fourth were killed.

From every window and balcony of the narrow street which then led up to the Baillie Guard Gate, a stream of bullets poured upon the gallant band. The Highlanders and Sikhs pushed on with Havelock and Outram at their head. Neill followed with his Madras Fusiliers, "charging," as has been said, "through a very tempest of fire." Even the women hurled down stones and furniture, and the flat roofs were filled with Sepoys, firing down into the street. Brave Neill fell, shot through the head, and many another hero was mown down; but the Baillie Guard was reached, and the garrison was saved.

There was a breach in the wall—the Baillie Guard itself was filled with earth—and Havelock and Outram pushed through this, followed by the eager soldiers, begrimed with dust and blood. The fighting men, the civilians, the women and children, rushed down to welcome their deliverers, and the Highlanders in the exuberance of their joy began to dance the Highland fling, until Havelock came out and put a stop to it.

Johnson was with the rear-guard, covering the spare ammunition and the wounded, and he joined the main force about four p.m. In the night, accompanied by his friend Dr. Greenhow—they had been together, it will be remembered, in the 1st Oude Cavalry—he went out to bring in as many wounded as he might find. They discovered a number of wounded men, whom they brought in, in the course of the night, on the horses, which were led by Johnson's troopers, and by this means many lives were saved, which would otherwise have been sacrificed. All who had been left behind disabled, would probably have died of their wounds before morning, or have fallen victims to the mutineers ; as indeed was the case next day, when about forty of the wounded unfortunately fell into the hands of the rebels and were butchered ; some killed with daggers, and some burnt to death.* Lieutenant Havelock,† who had been wounded, as we have seen, at the Charbagh bridge, and who was in one of the dhoolies, had a narrow escape of his life. Johnson did his best to get the Victoria Cross for his friend Dr. Greenhow for this action. He made no claim for himself, and neither of them received it.

Marshman, in his " Life of Havelock," refers to this rescue.‡ " The rear-guard, consisting of the 90th, under Colonel Campbell, had been left with two of the heavy guns at the Motee Mahal, to aid the advance of the 78th Highlanders, who had, apparently unknown to them, taken a different path, and joined the main body under the generals. With this rear-

---

* It was not until daylight the following morning that Lieutenant Johnson became aware that these wounded men had been left in the Motee Mahal itself, but he and Surgeon Greenhow had brought in about twenty, all they could find.

† Now General Sir Henry Havelock, V.C., etc.

‡ So also Mr. Archibald Forbes, " Havelock," p. 208.

guard were the spare ammunition and the wounded. During the night of the 25th, Lieutenant Johnson, whose brilliant charge in the action at the Alumbagh has already been mentioned, dismounted half his troop of Irregular Cavalry, and issuing forth from the Residency with the led horses, proceeded of his own accord in the direction of the Motee Mahal to bring in as many wounded as he might find. He discovered no trace of any enemy in any direction, and it is probable that if advantage could have been taken of this circumstance, which unhappily was not known, the whole of the rear-guard, with the guns, the ammunition, and the wounded, might have reached the Residency before the morning in safety, and the unhappy loss, which partially dimmed the triumph of the day, would have been avoided."

Johnson wrote the following letter to his mother during the siege:

"Tehri Kothi,* 9th Nov., 1857.

"I head this the Tehri Kothi, thinking that long ere this you will have a map of Lucknow before you,

* The Tehree Kothee, which was captured on 26th September, is still standing. It is a fine mansion just outside the Residency walls, and near the Baillie Guard Gate, as after the first relief the defences were extended.

and am writing on the 9th November, so that it may be ready to send out the moment there is an opportunity of its reaching Cawnpore. On the 6th a man came in from Bruce, the superintendent of police, at Cawnpore, saying Sir Colin Campbell, with 5000 bayonets, 600 cavalry, and 36 guns, would be at Alumbagh on the 10th, so we may expect now to be relieved in a few days.

"We have now been shut up here since the 25th September, a day which will be celebrated in my memory as the most thoroughly unsatisfactory one I ever passed in my life. What made it so annoying was our being mauled so in the town by an enemy so cowardly in the open. All the cavalry had orders to accompany the rear-guard and the baggage, and we came along very well as far as the Charbagh bridge, when instead of continuing along the straight road to the Baillie Guard, we turned sharp to the right, along the edge of the canal. Then we had the canal —a deep, perpendicular cutting, about thirty feet deep, and nearly dry at the bottom—on our right, and high fields, houses, hedges, and enclosures of all sorts to our left; the road choked up at intervals with commissariat carts, shot carts, camels, and bullocks ; the *tout ensemble* making it rather a lively sort of place for cavalry to work in, as you may imagine. This manœuvre would have done very well had it been determined to make a dash for the ¡Baillie Guard by this route with infantry alone, which I have no doubt would have been accomplished with little loss. But the road or track was narrow, uneven, and soft ; just the sort of place for heavy guns and baggage to get in a fix. Let me tell you here the guns we had with us were some of them long iron eighteen-pounder siege guns, and an eighteen-inch howitzer, with twenty bullocks to each ; and unless in a city where there are large enough streets to work and turn in, they become worse than useless.

"Well, here we were in the lane, being potted at from all directions among the enclosures, from every corner, window, and hedge about the place, without being able to see where the bullets came from so as to return shot or charge the villains. The rest of the column were by this time about two miles ahead of us, and after being shot at for about three hours, we got the carts to move on, and came along the lanes and enclosures till we reached the leading division about four p.m.

"We came through a terrible fire, and it was coming up one of these lanes that poor Warren, my adjutant, was shot dead through the heart close to me. He was riding alongside of me. He died instantaneously; he was a dead man before he reached the ground. I jumped off my horse and put him in a dhooly that was passing at the time, and told the bearers to hurry on with him to the front as fast as they could. This little business very nearly cost me my life, for on getting on my horse again I found I was the last in the lane, and a body of the enemy firing straight into me, at about sixty yards. I was in hopes I should have recovered his body, but I never could find it again. I greatly feel his loss, and though I had only been with him about a month, we were great friends. He was a man I could always trust to do any duty for me, and he always did it cheerfully and well. Besides, he was an excellent companion, and always in good spirits. I shall have the painful duty of writing the last account of him to his father. His death will be a great blow to them, for he was evidently a great favourite with them, as well as with his regiment out here. Since his death I have another man, Hay, of the 28th, now doing duty with the Engineers, appointed in his place. I knew him when I was in Lucknow before, and we shall get on well together. General Outram had promised him an appointment, and I asked him to let him come to me as adjutant, which he has sanctioned. He is a quiet, gentlemanly fellow, and I have great faith in him. I am also fortunate in having appointed to me, as doctor, an old friend of mine—Greenhow, of the 1st Oude Cavalry that was. But as yet these appointments have to be confirmed by the Commander-in-Chief.

"On our arrival here, on the 25th September, we found the garrison not nearly in the state of starvation we had been given to suppose. The ladies and children looked pale and sickly, which one might expect, for although I don't pretend to be well up in babies' food, I fancy tough beef and chupatties are not quite the food for delicate females and growing children. After we had been in Lucknow a few days we found ourselves besieged and unable to get out. Hardinge, Barrow, and I, all tried one night with our various detachments to get out, but we found the fire so heavy that we were compelled to return. Had we gone on, about half of us only would probably have reached Alumbagh, certainly not more. The ground was not such that one could have made a gallop for it, and cut one's self out, or we should have done it, and the enemy were shooting at us all the time in all directions. Thus we came back, and our horses have been starving to death, eating one another's tails off, as they did in the

Crimea. Poor brutes! it is quite melancholy to see them. As for ourselves, we get beef and wheat enough to eat, but no other luxuries. I thrive wonderfully upon it, being in excellent health, have nearly got rid of the pain in my side, and diarrhœa. The weather and the water are beautiful. The former, with the excitement, has set me up, I expect.

"Never was there such an extraordinary siege as this, I should think—the way the little garrison has held out against the thousands and thousands that have been trying to take it. The place, I think, would doubtless have fallen, had it not been for the number of officers shut up in proportion to the men. They certainly deserve any amount of praise that can be given to them. The shaves and narrow escapes from death are extraordinary. One man, an officer, is now going about with a bullet in his brain and doing well—the name, I think, is Charlton. Another officer was looking out for a shot through an embrasure one day, when the enemy fired a twenty-four-pounder full of grape right into him ; his clothes were cut to pieces in four places, a bit of his ear, and some of his hair cut off. Of course he was knocked over and stunned, but he got up and shook himself in half an hour, and was on duty again next day. Some of our men occasionally make good shots with the Enfield. One of the 90th made a very good shot once, and picked off a native swell (one of importance, apparently) as he was reading a proclamation to his men on parade before an attack.

" The enemy fired all sorts of things : sometimes telegraph wire rolled up into the shape of a shot ; sometimes a couple of brickbats ; several logs of wood ; sometimes balls of wood (they did little or no damage, but made a great illumination and noise, as they came over), sometimes pieces of shell. My horse has been wounded three times since he has been in here. Up to to-day I have been fortunate in not having been touched myself, nor had I any very narrow shaves. Several round shots have come into our room. One came and lodged in a bag of rupees in a treasure chest, just at the foot of my bed, one evening, as we were all talking quietly just before turning in. The next day another, a nine-pounder, came in like a flash of lightning. First it came through a room full of women and children and servants of all sorts ; then through the next door ; then through one of the legs of our mess table, and was brought up at the opposite wall : all the damage it did was bruising one lady's legs.

Another we had in the middle of the night from the same gun cut a man's (Hall's) pillow clean in two as he was lying fast asleep in bed, not hurting him in the least. Another came through the tumbril just outside the door, and on through the verandah full of my men, and never hurt one of them. Two ladies were shot during the siege, and lots of children.

" I continue my letter to-day, the 12th. We have established a telegraph between this and Alumbagh. It told us to-day that the Chief had arrived this morning, and would march on the Dilkoosha the day after to-morrow (the 14th). I wish he was coming the direct route, but dare say it's all for the best, and will end well.

" Some of the prices during the siege will amuse you. Cheroots (small ones) sold for two rupees each (4s.); a couple of flannel shirts sold for £7 10s.; a pot of treacle, £4 16s. I bought ten candles one day for 26s., and thought myself very lucky to get them. Coarse sugar, 32s. a pound; brandy, 80s. a bottle (a man gave a watch one day for a glass of brandy). One pound of rice, 8s. My russeldar (a native officer) had difficulty in getting a leaf of native tobacco for a rupee. The men were reduced to smoking tea-leaves and dried leaves of trees.

We are to be on full rations again from to-morrow, but grog and tobacco are what we want most, and there are none. I am happy to tell you there are only 550 sick and wounded to-day; they did badly up to the 3rd November, when suddenly a change for the better came over them, and they have been doing well ever since. Nearly all the cases of amputation have died; in fact, the slaughter has been awful, and, what is worse, there appear to have been many of the wounded left behind, who fell into the hands of the rebels.

"I sent several letters out during the siege; the last I sent was sewn up in the sole of a man's shoe; probably none ever reached, as the enemy kept a sharp look-out, and boned most of the men, who were made to work in their trenches. You will have heard of the action at Alumbagh, two days before we came here, so I won't give you a second edition, except to remark that it was ludicrous the way the enemy bolted, leaving their guns in different places, for us to take. The mare I was riding there was shot through the hock by grape.

"No one, I think, anticipated the amount of opposition we had coming in here, and it appears that Nana Sing, one of the leading men in Oude, joined the rebels the day before we came in. Nearly

O

the whole of the country (Oude) is up against us now: so much for annexation! I think there must be at least fifty thousand armed men fighting against us here now.

"*November* 14*th.*—Sir Colin Campbell has advanced to-day as far as Dilkoosha and the Martinière. They did not appear to have much fighting, which I am glad of, for we have had quite enough slaughter already. I forgot to tell you in the former part of this letter that my name has gone in for a Brevet Majority, as soon as I get my captaincy. General Havelock sent my name in quite unexpectedly to me, but I should have got it anyhow, I think. This will have to be put in orders at the Horse Guards, and I must get Charlie or Freddy * to see this is done, otherwise it will be left out. The Crimea, Lucknow, and Eyre's despatch, ought to give me the Brevet Majority at once, and I think Jem Macdonald would think so too. I shall be anxiously looking out for two months' English letters to-morrow.

"*November* 15*th, morning.*—Sir Colin Campbell did not appear to advance yesterday: probably they were making a road across the canal. We are put on full rations again, and my poor horses are to have

* The late Hon. Frederick Craven.

two pounds of barley each in future. Heavy firing guns heard in the direction of Dilkoosha; our own guns, I think, perhaps smashing a few houses before they advance. The enemy also made an attack on us, but then their attacks appear to consist in making a tremendous fire through loopholes and windows. They will find some difference in the way we make an attack (sortie) to-day. The worst of all this firing at night on their part is, it obliges us to sleep in our clothes, and always to be ready to turn out at a moment's notice, in case they could get up their pluck enough to come on properly. I hope Sir Colin Campbell will come in with less loss than we did, and leave none of his wounded behind.

"*November* 19*th*, 9 *p.m.*—Just time to finish this. We opened a communication with Sir Colin Campbell yesterday: all the sick and wounded move out to-night. Not a moment for any more: no letters in yet, but we are very anxious for them."

In the early part of his letter, Johnson says that so far he had had no very narrow shaves; so it must have been just afterwards that he had the following wonderful escape. He was standing at a window out of which the panes of glass had been blown, and was looking through his telescope for the coming in of Sir Colin Campbell; and as he leant against the wooden frame (only two or three inches wide) in the centre of the window, one of the enemy took a quiet "pot" at him. The bullet lodged in the narrow bit of wood behind which he was standing; he fell back from the shock, but was quite unhurt.

When the history of this heroic relief and defence became known, Lord Canning, the Governor-General of India, wrote of the besieged garrison: "The despatches show how thoroughly that gallant band has sustained the reputation of British soldiers for daring, discipline, and determination, whether in the plain, in the hand-to-hand struggle, in the street-fighting, or in the more wearying labours of the siege. His Lordship in Council acknowledges with pleasure the cheerful alacrity with which Captain Barrow, commanding Volunteer Cavalry, Captains Johnson and Hardynge, commanding Irregular Cavalry, have come forward to volunteer their services on every opportunity."

Sir James Outram's despatch shows how fully he appreciated the spirit of his men:

"*Alumbagh, November 25th*, 1857. — I cannot conclude this report without expressing to his Excellency my intense admiration of the noble spirit displayed by all ranks and grades of the force, since we entered Lucknow. Themselves placed in a state of siege, suddenly reduced to scanty and unsavoury rations, denied all the little luxuries, such as tea, sugar, rum, which, by constant use, had been to them almost necessaries of life; smitten in many cases by the same scorbutive affections, and other evidences of debility, which obtained among the original garrison; compelled to engage in laborious operations, exposed to constant danger, and kept ever on the alert; their spirits and cheerfulness, zeal and discipline, seemed to rise with the occasion. Never could there have been a force more free from grumblers, more cheerful, more willing, or more earnest. Amongst the sick and wounded this glorious spirit was, if possible, still more conspicuous than among those fit for duty. It was a painful sight to see so many noble fellows maimed and suffering, and denied those comforts of which they stood so much in need; but it was truly delightful, and made one proud of his countrymen, to observe the heroic fortitude and hearty cheerfulness with which all was borne.* . . . Captain Barrow, commanding Volunteer Cavalry, Captains Johnson and Hardynge, commanding Irregular Cavalry, though precluded from acting in their proper capacity, have

---

* Here follows a list of those to whom the General offers his acknowledgments for their services during the siege.

regularly volunteered for every service in which they or their men could be useful, and have maintained posts or furnished working parties with cheerful alacrity."

The high opinion of Captain Johnson expressed above by Sir James Outram was repeated some years later by his Chief of the Staff, Colonel Napier, afterwards Field-Marshal Lord Napier of Magdala, who wrote in 1865 the following statement of Captain Johnson's services :—

"Major W. T. Johnson was in command of a squadron of the 12th Irregular Cavalry in Outram's advance on Lucknow.

"During this advance Major Johnson particularly distinguished himself in an action with a body of rebels who were defeated and destroyed by a force under Colonel Vincent Eyre, also in action with the enemy at Alumbagh.

"On entering the Residency he dismounted his men, and brought in a number of wounded on the led horses.

"Major Johnson and his squadron were shut in with the garrison during the remainder of the siege, and assisted in all the duties of the defence.

"I am aware that the late Sir James Outram held the highest opinion of Major Johnson as a gallant and excellent cavalry officer, and I am sure would have given him a much more valuable testimonial than mine, were he living.

"Major Johnson served with Her Majesty's 20th Regiment in the Crimea, and with the Scinde Horse in Persia.

"I beg to recommend him most strongly for any military employment in England that may be available, in which his energy and skill as a cavalry officer would render him valuable."

The following was also written, some years later, by Lord Napier, when Major Johnson was seeking a nomination for the Navy for one of his sons.

"June 24th, 1876.

"Major Johnson, formerly of the Indian Service, has distinguished himself both in India and the Crimea as a gallant and able soldier. The testimonial which was given to him by the officer commanding Her Majesty's 20th Regiment, for his gallant conduct at Inkerman, is one of which any soldier of his standing might be proud. He was a volunteer attached to a British regiment, and rendered essential service in the battle, in which ten officers of the regiment were killed and wounded.

"Major Johnson's services were equally distinguished

in the mutiny of the Indian army. General Sir James Outram held him in the highest estimation. A reference to Major Johnson's record of services will show what a very strong claim he has on the public service. He was obliged to leave the army on account of having sacrificed his health in the public service."

CHAPTER XII.

THE SECOND RELIEF AND EVACUATION OF THE
RESIDENCY.   NOVEMBER 9-22, 1857.

ON the 9th November, the day on which Johnson
began the long letter from the Tehree Kothee, Outram heard that Sir Colin Campbell was within a march
of Alumbagh.   On the evening of that day, Mr. T.
Kavanagh, an officer of the uncovenanted service,
volunteered to go from the Residency to the camp at
Alumbagh, and take important plans and papers from
Sir James Outram to Sir Colin Campbell.   He was
accordingly disguised as a "badmash," or sepoy
mutineer, and got to the British camp very early the
next morning, having gone right through the enemy's
pickets, and through the very middle of the rebels.
It was a very brave act, as he ran the risk of being
crucified or cruelly tortured, if discovered.   He had
some very thrilling adventures, but accomplished his
mission successfully, and received the Victoria Cross.

There was a celebrated spy in the Residency called Runjeet Singh, who used to go out and get information for the garrison as to the movements outside. This man accompanied Kavanagh when he was sent with the papers to the Alumbagh. One day Runjeet Singh came back with the news that a regiment of women had arrived, who played something under their arms! These were, of course, the Highlanders, with their kilts and bagpipes.

On the 14th November Sir Colin Campbell arrived at the Dilkoosha Palace. Sir James Outram had recommended him to "give the city a wide berth," so he took the extended route, halted for the night and the following day, and sent a message from the semaphore on the Martinière: "Advance to-morrow." On the morrow, the 16th, the relieving column accordingly advanced up the right bank of the Goomtee river, and attacked the Secundrabagh with heavy fighting. The next day, the 17th, the advance to Lucknow went on with stubborn resistance all the way; stronghold after stronghold fell; and after severe fighting the Motee Munzil and the Motee Mahal were taken, and Lieutenant, now Field-Marshal Lord Roberts, hoisted the flag of the 2nd Punjab Infantry on the top of the mess-house to show Outram and Havelock where they were. It was near this that the meeting took place of Sir Colin Campbell, Outram, and Havelock, which is represented in the celebrated picture, and the second and final relief of Lucknow was therefore accomplished on the afternoon of the 17th November, 1857.

The sick and wounded, and the women and children, were removed to Dilkoosha Palace during the night of the 19th November, and the remainder of the garrison were taken there at midnight on the 22nd, when in deep silence the Residency was evacuated. The whole force reached the Dilkoosha Palace about dawn on the 23rd. One officer only was left behind. He was asleep in a retired spot, and his friends did not miss him. He awoke to find himself alone, as all the troops had marched away. He fled at once, passing through thousands of mutineers (who did not know that the Residency had been abandoned), and in time he overtook the rear-guard in safety.

The relief was overshadowed by an irreparable loss. On the 20th November General Havelock had been attacked with dysentery. His constitution was already shattered by privation and fatigue; the symptoms grew rapidly worse, and on the morning of the 24th he passed away, at the Dilkoosha Palace. " I have so ruled my life, that when death came I might face it without fear :" these were among his last words.

In the afternoon of the same day, shortly after his death, the troops marched to Alumbagh, taking his body on a litter. The next morning he was buried, near a mango tree, on which he had carved, a little time before, the letter H. The tree is still standing beside the memorial.

Johnson's health had for a long time been failing ; it was only out of sheer pluck that he had gone on so long. It now gave way completely, and after the march to the Alumbagh he was very dangerously ill. His old friend and comrade, Dr. H. M. Greenhow, who was with him there throughout his illness, and attended him with the greatest kindness, wrote the letter to Colonel Turner * at this time.

"Camp Alumbagh, near Lucknow,
"December 11th, 1857.

"I am asked by my friend Johnson, of the 6th Bombay Native Infantry, and now commanding the 12th Irregular Cavalry, to write to you, and inform you that he is at present unable to send you a line himself on account of sickness. What he wishes particularly to say is, that he wrote to his mother in England, as soon as Sir Colin Campbell relieved

* Johnson's cousin.   Afterwards Major-General Turner.

Lucknow, about a fortnight ago, but that he is un-
certain whether the letter may not have miscarried, as
we know several dáks have done. Should the letter
not reach, Johnson would feel that his mother had not
heard for a long time, and he would therefore be glad
if you could kindly let her know that he is safe out of
Lucknow. We are now within five miles of the city,
encamped in the open plain, and in a few weeks shall
no doubt commence operations on it. Sir Colin
Campbell, after relieving it, went back to Cawnpore,
where he has been dispersing the Gwalior Contingent.

"At present I am sorry to say Johnson is very far
from well; indeed, for the last ten days he has been
laid up with remittent fever, and he is much weakened
by it. I trust he will soon take a favourable change,
but his knocking about in Persia was but a bad pre-
paration for this campaign in Oude. Johnson asks
me to tell you his name has gone in for a Brevet
Majority."

Colonel Turner, in forwarding the above letter to
Enborne, wrote from Bombay : "You will see Billy's
name in all the despatches, and in Lord Canning's
general orders. He is a noble fellow, and his rela-
tions must all be proud of him, but I wish he were
here instead of where he is. He seems to be in
kind hands."

A short time afterwards Johnson wrote to his mother in a very trembling hand :

"Alumbagh, December 28, 1857.

" Don't be alarmed at this horribly groggy writing, but it is better than writing by deputy, and it will show you how much better I am. I am thankful to say I have been getting so much stronger the last few days; in fact, I only take now four grains of quinine a day. But I have just pulled through a very serious illness, and the doctors were very much alarmed about me at one time. They are going to send me home immediately I am strong enough to move. This I feel I am obliged to give in to, especially as my health in India has of late been failing me so much. Do you remember my mentioning in one of my letters that I thought I should last as far as Lucknow? Well, I *have* lasted as far, and am now obliged to give in. It is a bad thing for me having to go away just now, as it will prevent my being present with my sowars at the taking of Lucknow. I expect the taking of Lucknow will not be very severe ; in fact, with the enormous force we are able to bring against it, I should think they will soon give in. I am sorry to come home before seeing the fellows punished.

"My name has gone in for a Brevet Majority on promotion to my company; Havelock sent it in. Poor old gentleman! I noticed a great change in him about a fortnight before he died. He and I were always very good friends, and I am heartily sorry he was not spared a few months longer, just to let him see how much the country appreciated his services. His despatch seems to have been lost, for we have never seen it published anywhere ; but it must turn up in time, for it was a despatch of much importance, containing an account of the first relief of Lucknow. How delightful it will be to see you all again, and to be once more at dear old Enborne!

"I must end this now, for I am very, very weak. I am just able to stand up to-day without support, but cannot walk yet. You have no idea how kind every one of my friends have been: some sending me grapes, some eggs (very difficult to get here), and MacPherson* of the Highlanders, an old friend of mine, sends me port-wine, grapes, and jelly. You would laugh if you saw the place I am living in ; but I am very comfortable. Dr. Greenhow, my old friend, is most kind and attentive ; in fact, I have never experienced so much attention from any one,

* Sir Herbert MacPherson.

and I hope some day I may have an opportunity to repay him. I can't give you the least idea when to look out for me in England, but I shall come overland, and will write you many letters before I start, I hope."

On the 30th January, 1858, Johnson wrote from Benares, to say that he was comparatively well again, and on his way to Calcutta. He was detained there on account of all the conveyances being taken up for the Governor-General; but he got to Calcutta in time to leave on the 23rd February by the *Nubia.*

He wrote from Calcutta:—

"I am thinking of going by Trieste if I can get a chance, and do a little Austria and Germany. I want to see some of the principal arsenals and reviews *en route*, if I can. I shall not delay very long, though. No English letters again; the postmasters either don't pass them on or the rebels bone them. I got an old letter a short time ago that had come to Bombay up the Indus, *viâ* Mooltan and Alumbagh, by way of a short cut to Calcutta. A letter from Alumbagh from my Adjutant, Hay, dated 15th, says: 'No fighting yet, but great preparations for the attack on Lucknow. The whole way to Cawnpore the road is covered with supplies and troops—the electric telegraph is into camp, and we begin to feel ourselves the masters of the country again. . . .' I am delighted at the idea of getting out of Calcutta."

His next letter to his mother was written on board the *Nubia*, 11th March, 1858:

"You will be glad to hear I passed the Medical Board in Calcutta with very little trouble—they made no hesitation about it whatever, after looking over my case; in fact, were awfully civil, and told me that my sickness having been contracted in the field, my leave at home should count as service. This was a bit of liberality on their part I was not prepared for, but they are tolerably lenient just now towards all those who were in Lucknow. My health is much better, fever all gone, but I have grown very old, and very yellow, and I have a feeling in my right side as if there were a nine-pound shot lodged in my liver. I'll try and jog it out, though, if I can, between Syracuse and Hamburg, and if some of the diligence travelling and bad roads between those two places don't succeed, I don't know what will. We are not coming *viâ* Marseilles this time, having seen enough of that route, but we are going to do Italy and Austria, starting from Sicily; Palermo probably or Catania, to Naples, Rome, Florence, Verona, Venice, Trieste, Vienna, Prague, as far as Dresden. At some of these places I hope to see some of the reviews,

P

and visit some of the principal arsenals; people too declare we should not miss the Holy Week in Rome, which they all say is the finest sight in the world. Young Birch and I hope De la Fosse will join our party—the same man that escaped from Cawnpore. The former came into Lucknow with us, and got a shot in the back, which gives him a good deal of trouble—pieces of bone still keep coming away; but with a little cooking up he'll do for the tour. My great chum, Jim Grant, remained behind at Madras, to stay a fortnight with his brother."

He carried out his programme, and arrived in England, April 19th. Shortly after his return he attended the Levee, and was presented by a connection by marriage.* He wore the medal and three clasps for the Crimea, the Turkish Crimean medal, the medal and clasp for Persia, and the medal and clasp for Lucknow; and being the only officer in either of the services who was engaged in all these three campaigns, he attracted the special notice of the Queen, for Lake wrote as follows to Mrs. Johnson, April 30th: "I have this moment received the commands of Her Majesty to tell her any circumstances relating to Billy which I may know, as she takes much interest in the Indian officers presented

* General Sir Atwell Lake, K.C.B. Died 1881.

to her, and has desired inquiries to be made respecting him. Will you, if Billy is with you, ask him to send me *instantly* a statement of his services. . . . Let him be explicit, for it is probable Her Majesty may send for me, and I should like to make out a good story for him. Let him tell of his Crimean and Persian Campaigns. I have but this moment received my orders from the Lord Chamberlain's office, or would sooner have sent to you." The statement of services was, of course, sent in with as little delay as possible, but Johnson was afterwards informed that it was too late to be laid before Her Majesty.

On the 13th June, 1860, Colonel Baker wrote from the India Office : " I have the satisfaction of informing you that Secretary Sir Charles Wood, having communicated with the General Commanding-in-Chief on the subject of your strong claims to receive the Brevet rank of major, in consideration of your services in the field from 1854 to the present time, has been informed that His Royal Highness, agreeably to Sir Charles Wood's recommendation, has submitted to the Secretary of State for War, that you should be promoted to the rank of major, with the date 5th March, 1860, the day after you became a captain regimentally."

He had come home on fifteen months' sic
certificate, but on the expiration of his furlough, t
examining physician, Sir James Ranald Mart:
certified that his health at that time would not allo
of his return to India, and that, if he went ba
he would die in two years. He applied, according
for a further extension of leave, but it was n
granted, and he had no option but to retire. Th
he did, after his marriage, September 18th, 18(
to Mary Amelia, only daughter of Thomas Poys
Esquire, of Wirksworth, Derbyshire.*

The volunteer movement was then just beginnir
and Major Johnson took a warm interest in it, a
early in 1861, was appointed to an adjutancy
volunteers at Liverpool. Colonel Adam Gladsto
then commanded the regiment. This appointme
he after some time resigned, and in 1865 went
live in North Wales, to manage the property of h
cousin, the late Mrs. Oakeley, of Tany Bwlch.
1871 he went from Wales to Berlin, at the terminati
of the Franco-German War, and was in Berlin at t

---

* Four sons and one daughter survive him. The eldest son, Cha
Blois, holds the livings of Enborne and Hampstead, in the gift of
Earl of Craven, of which his grandfather and uncle were rectors.
second, Francis William Blois, is an officer in the P. & O. Servi
The third, Thomas Gordon Blois, is a lieutenant in the 22nd Pun
Infantry. The fourth, John Ernest Blois, is lieutenant in the Gui
Cavalry.

triumphal entry in June, and had interviews with the Crown Prince and Princess, and, what he was most anxious for, one with Count von Moltke. Throughout his life he took the keenest interest in his profession, and was always attracted by anything connected with it. On his wedding tour, during the great struggle of Italy, he and his wife witnessed the siege of Gaeta, and the triumphal entry into Naples of the King of Italy and Garibaldi, to whom they were presented afterwards.

In 1872 he made a tour round the coast of England, to survey it, with a view of making a second line of defence by means of gunboats. The observations he made, and his ideas on the subject, are embodied in a pamphlet he afterwards wrote, called " Gunboats for Volunteers."

The latter years of Major Johnson's life were spent at Seaford, in Sussex, where he eventually settled in 1881, and built himself a house. He used generally to attend the Lucknow Anniversary Dinner, on the 25th September, and in 1893, when he was no longer amongst the survivors, and the chairman, Sir William Olpherts, proposed the " memory of our departed comrades," the name of Johnson was mentioned, together with those of Havelock, Outram, Neill, Inglis, Napier, and other true and faithful servants who had entered into their rest. He attended the funeral of the last-named old friend in St. Paul's, and was invited to that of him, who wrote of Lucknow—

> " Hold it for fifteen days ! We have held it for eighty-seven !
> And ever upon the topmost roof, the banner of England blew."

For some little time before the end, Major Johnson's memory had been affected, the result, the doctors said, of a blow on the side of his head —probably a sabre cut received in action, which, in the excitement of the moment, had perhaps hardly been noticed, but which took effect many years after. He died at Seaford, on May 31st, 1893 ; and with the flag of England, which he loved so well, as his pall, he was laid to rest on June 3rd, in the quiet churchyard of the little Cinque Port, followed by those who loved him, and by a contingent of the 1st Sussex Volunteer Royal Engineers, and a party of the Coast-guards, who asked to be allowed to show him this last mark of respect.

A small brass tablet, with a summary of his services, has been placed to his memory in the chancel of the Memorial Church at Lucknow ; it is close to the monument of General Barrow, with whom he fought on the march to the first Relief, and to that of his late chief, Sir James Outram, for whom he had ever a profound admiration and regard.

The name of the regiment he commanded at Lucknow—the 12th Irregular Cavalry—is engraved on the pedestal of Havelock's monument in Trafalgar Square. In front of the monument are the words which were spoken by the General after the Battle of Bithoor :

"Soldiers, your labours, your privations, your sufferings, and your valour, will not be forgotten by a grateful country."

THE END.

PRINTED BY WILLIAM CLOWES AND SONS, LIMITED, LONDON AND BECCLES.

www.ingramcontent.com/pod-product-compliance
Lightning Source LLC
Chambersburg PA
CBHW021226020726
47498CB00008B/2717